Thirst Quencher
Every Woman Needs That One

Thirst Quencher
Every Woman Needs That One

BY

TRACY WILSON

http://beautifulpublications.com

Published by
Beautiful Publications LLC
Stratford, CT 06614

This book is a work of fiction. Names, characters, places, and incidents are either products of the author's imagination or are used fictitiously. Any resemblance to actual events or locales or persons, living or dead, is entirely coincidental.

PRINT ISBN: 978-1-7343353-6-1
EBOOK ISBN: 978-1-7343353-7-8

Printed in the United States of America

Chapter 1 - Alexis (Lexi)

"Dammn!" Lexi panted...

"Are you satisfied?"

"Yes my Thirst Quencher..." she breathed...

"Will that be cash or charge?"

"Both..."

"Both?"

"Yes – use my card for the fee – I'll tip you in cash..." she said as she handed me her Black Card..."

"Yes Maam..."

"Lexi..."

"Yes Lexi..."

"I need to ask you something..." she said as she sat up and handed me the envelope...

"Yes Lexi?"

"Will you marry me?"

"Lexi..." I said as I pulled her up into my arms and kissed her... "That's very sweet – I'm humbled... but..."

"Sterling – just hear me out..."

"I'm listening..."

"What if I told you that you could keep your job?"

"Lexi – you'd do that? Are you serious?"

"Yes my Thirst Quencher..." she breathed as she kissed me...

"Lexi... I can't..."

"Why not?"

"Because... when I get married... I want to be with my wife exclusively..."

"And when is that going to be?"

"I don't know..."

"You're enjoying this – aren't you?"

"No Lexi... I'm not..."

"Why not?"

"I'm not sure what you're asking me..."

"I'm asking you to be my husband..."

"If I were going to marry anyone... it would be you..." I breathed as I pulled her into a kiss...

"Marry me then..."

"You're willing to be my wife... and let me keep my job?"

"Sterling – you work a couple of hours each day – you make good money – plus tips – hell yea I'm willing to be your wife and let you keep your job!"

"So you want me for my money – is that it?"

"My Thirst Quencher..." she breathed as she pulled me into a kiss... "I want you... for you..."

"So if I told you I would quit my job you'd still want me?"

"Hell yea..." she breathed as she pulled me down on top of her....

"Lexi... I need to go..."

"I know..." she breathed as she pulled my face to hers and pushed her tongue in my mouth...

"Lexi... I... have... another... appointment..."

"Fuck her..."

"Lexi... I'm sorry..." I said as I got up...

"Fine..." she sighed...

"I'll come back when I get off work..." I said as I opened the door and walked out. Thank God this next appointment was my last because I couldn't stop thinking about Lexi. I've been with lots of women but Lexi was special. Whenever I'm with her I never feel like we're just fucking – I always feel like we're making love...

Chapter 2 - LaShonda

"You're late..." she said as I walked in...

"I'm sorry..." I breathed as I pulled her into a kiss and held her...

"I pay you in advance, I tip you well – I expect to get what I pay for..."

"I'll make it up to you... I promise..." I said as I took off my clothes. I couldn't stand this Ghetto Ratchet Hood Bitch. She met her husband in high school – he was a virgin and when they started dating and he finally got some pussy it was pretty much over for him after that – he didn't have any other experience so he did the best he could in bed but LaShonda was too selfish to take the time to teach him what he needed to do to please her so one thing led to another, I fucked her, and now I'm her Thirst Quencher. It took everything in me to fuck her - her breath stinks, her pussy stinks, her titties sag – and don't get me started on her make-up – but she pays in advance, she tips well, and I get an extra $500 for anal – so I had to man up and get to work...

"Bring your ass here..." she said as she grabbed me by my dick and wrapped her lips around it. As much as I couldn't stand her ass – her head game was on point – even with a condom...

"Who am I?" I growled as I began fucking her mouth...

"My... Thirst... Quencher..." she answered as best she could. She continued slobbing and sucking until I got hard and then she spoke... "Okay – I'm ready..." she breathed as she lay back on the bed and spread her legs. The thought of going down on her made me gag but as I got closer to her pussy I could tell she douched...

"Thank God..." I said as I put the dental damn on her pussy and my tongue went to work...

"Oooohhh... Yes.... Fuck..."

"You like that?"

"Yes my Thirst Quencher – yes!" I went back to work on her clit with my tongue as I spread her lips and inserted two fingers in her ass and my thumb in her pussy... "Yes! Don't stop! Oh God! I'm cumming! Aaaaah!" I continued to put in work as she had multiple orgasms and then she tried to push me away from her... "My Thirst Quencher... stop... I can't take anymore..."

"Take it!" I growled and then I sucked her clit hard...

"Aaaah! Oh God! I'm cumming again!" she screamed as her legs clamped around my head and she dug her nails into my shoulders... "MY THIRST QUENCHERRRRR!!!" she screamed as her body rose up off the bed and then she fell back down. I came up between her legs and thrust myself inside her before she had a chance to recover... "Fuck me! Just like that! Yeessss!"

"Who am I?" I growled as I pounded her pussy...

"My Thirst Quencher!" she moaned...

"Damn right I am!" I growled as I continued pounding her...

"I'm cumming... I'm cumming... I'm cumming... I'M CUMMING! AAAAAGGGHHH!"

"Get on your hands and knees..." I commanded...

"Yes my Thirst Quencher!" she breathed as she jumped up and got on her hands and knees... "Grab the headboard!" I commanded...

"Yes my Thirst Quencher!" she breathed. I put the lubricant on, stroked my dick... and waited... "Please..."

"Please what?" I growled as I spread her cheeks with the tip of my dick and grabbed her hair...

"Please – fuck my ass!"

"As you wish..." I breathed as I eased my dick in her ass...

"Yes my Thirst Quencher – give it to me!" I grabbed her by the waist and let her throw her ass back on my dick as I smacked it...

"Yes! Fuck my ass!" she moaned as she continued throwing her ass back on my dick and I increased the intensity of my slaps, alternating between each cheek... "Oh God! Fuck my ass! Just like that! I'M CUMMING! AAAGGGHHH!" She continued to throw her ass on my dick for a few moments and then she slowed down...

"I'm not done!" I growled as I grabbed her waist and began fucking her ass again...

"My Thirst Quencher..." she moaned...

"Yes... Your Thirst Quencher..." I growled as I increased my pace... I was ready to come... and I was also ready to go... "UUUGGGHHH!" I stayed in her ass until my dick went limp and then I pulled out before the condom could come off...

"Damn my Thirst Quencher – what the fuck got into you?" she asked as she turned around and lay back on the bed...

"Are you pleased?"

"Hell yea I'm pleased – you earned your money today..." she breathed as she lit a cigarette. I couldn't stand that shit. I can never get the smell outta my clothes – let alone my car – but this was my job – and it was pay day – so I had to be nice...

"Thank you..."

"Oh no – thank you!" she exclaimed as she handed me an envelope...

"You're welcome..." I said as I bent down to pick up the condom and headed towards the bathroom...

"Where you goin'?"

"I'ma flush these down the toilet..."

"You don't need to do that – I'm not gonna push them up inside me – I ain't tryin' to explain a baby to my husband!" she laughed...

"That's exactly what you'd do..." I thought to myself – but again – this was my job – and I had to be nice... "I flush them so you won't have any explaining to do..." I said as I flushed it down the toilet along with the dental damn...

"Whatchu mean?"

"I flush them so your husband doesn't find them in the garbage..."

"Oh shit – you right – I never thought of that!" she laughed as I got dressed...

"Same time next week?" I asked as I pulled her into a kiss...

"Same time next week..." she breathed as she kissed me back...

"Have a good day..." I said as I opened the door and then I left. As soon as I got to the elevator, I took the Listerine out of my pocket, opened it, poured it in my mouth, swished it around, spit in the garbage, threw the empty bottle in behind the spit, and got on the elevator...

Chapter 3 - Lexi

"Hey..." Lexi breathed as I came in...

"Hey..." I sighed. Lexi came over to me, turned me to face her, threw her arms around my neck, and kissed me...

"Talk to me..."

"I don't wanna talk..." I breathed as I kissed her...

"Mmmm... you used Listerine..."

"I did..."

"Come to bed..."

"Lexi... no..."

"No?"

"I need to get in the shower..." I said as I started taking my clothes off...

"Let me help you..."

"Lexi – stop!"

"Okay..." she whispered as she teared up...

"I'm sorry – I just came from an appointment – I want to get outta these clothes and take a shower..."

"Okay..." she sighed as she went to sit on the bed and sulk. I picked up my clothes, dropped them in the hamper, and got in the shower. As much as I hated it, I knew she wouldn't like what I had to say when I got out – but I also knew I had to do it... "Are you okay?"

"I'm fine – I'll be out in a few minutes..." I answered as I dried myself off and came out of the bathroom. I put on my robe, put on my slippers, and sat down on the bed... "Lexi – I can't do this..."

"Sterling – what are you saying?"

"I can't be in a relationship with you, sleep with other women, and then come back here and sleep with you as if I didn't just get finished fucking another woman..."

"Sterling..." she whispered as she teared up...

"Lexi – I'm sorry..."

"I'm not..."

"You're not? I don't understand..."

"You can't do it anymore because you love me..."

"Yes..." I said as I pulled her into a kiss... "I love you..."

"I love you too..."

"When I was with LaShonda – all I could do was think about you..."

"LaShonda?"

"Shit!"

"Oh hell no!"

"Lexi – I can explain..."

"You don't have to explain – I knew you were an escort – a Thirst Quencher – my Thirst

Quencher – but LaShonda? Aaaa Haaa! Aaaa Haaa!"

"What's so funny?"

"I went to school with that Bitch – she was a fuckin' snot – she wouldn't give me the time of day – she got married to an executive at IBM – far as I know she's still married – oh this is good! Aaaa Haaa! Aaaa Haaa!"

"Lexi! You can't repeat what I told you! I've spend years building my business! You'll ruin me!"

"I'm not going to repeat what you told me – but that Bitch is going to pay..."

"Lexi! No!"

"Oh yea – I'm going to meet up with her and we're going to have a conversation..."

"Lexi – please..."

"Sterling – you don't understand – she treated me like shit!"

"Lexi – please don't do this – you'll ruin me!"

"Sterling – I'm not going to ruin you – I do want to have a conversation with her though..."

"Why do you insist on a conversation with her? Why can't you just leave it alone?"

"Because she needs to be knocked down off her pedestal..."

"I wish I never said her name..." I sighed...

"I'm glad you did!" she laughed...

"Lexi – before I left – you asked me to marry you – I just told you I've been thinking about you – why can't we talk about that?"

"Okay – I'm sorry – I won't say anything..." Lexi said as she kissed me...

"You promise?"

"I can't promise you I'll never say anything to her – but I can promise you I won't say anything to her right now – I don't want to ruin you..."

"Thank you..." I breathed...

"So... you said you couldn't stop thinking about me..." she breathed as she pulled me down on top of her...

"Yeeesss..." I breathed as I spread her legs...

"I've been thinking about you too..." she breathed as I eased myself inside her...

"Is this what you were thinking?" I asked as I started thrusting...

"Yes my Thirst Quencher... Yes..." I pulled Lexi to me, kissed her hard, pushed my tongue in her mouth, spread her legs, and fucked her deeper... "Mmmm.... Mmmm.... Mmmm.... Mmmm...."

"Mmmph... Mmmph... Mmmph... Mmmph..." Lexi's body started to tense up and she dug her fingers in my ass as she pulled me in deeper... "Yes... Fuck me... Don't stop... Right there..."

"Cum for meee...."

"Aaagh... Aaagh... Aaagh... Aaagh... AAAAAGGGGHHHHH!"

"Uuugh! Uuugh! Uuugh! Uuugh! Uuugh! UUUUGGGGHHHH!!!" Lexi pulled my face to hers and we continued kissing for a few moments... "Yes..." I breathed...

"Yes?"

"Yes..."

"Oh Sterling!" she exclaimed as she started crying...

"Lexi..." I whispered as I kissed her tears...

"I can't wait to be your wife..."

"I'm going to be your husband..." I breathed as I kissed her... "And your Thirst Quencher..." I breathed as we continued kissing and went for round two...

Chapter 4 - Bazil

"This is Bazil..."
"Bazil – this is Sterling..."
"Sterling?"
"You don't remember me?"
"I remember you..." he sighed...
"What's wrong?"
"Sterling – what can I do for you?"
"I have a proposition for you..."
"I'm not interested..."
"Meet me at Thirty Three – my treat..."
"What time?"
"6 p.m..."
"I need to check with my wife..."
"Wife? You're married?"
"Yea – I'm married..."
"Congratulations..."
"Thank you..."
"You ready?" Beautiee asked...
"A friend reached out – he wants to catch up..."
"Oh that's nice – is he married?"
"I have no idea – why?"
"If he's married, we can go out sometime..."
"You don't mind?"

"I don't mind – the kids will – but I don't..." she breathed as she pulled him into a kiss...

"I love you..."

"I love you too..." she said as she went towards the door to leave... "Oh – Bazil?"

"Yes Beautiee?"

"Don't keep me waiting..." she said as she left...

"That was your wife?"

"Oh shit – I forgot you were on the phone!" Bazil laughed...

"How long have you been married?"

"I'll meet you at Thirty Three..." Bazil said as he hung up and hurried out to the parking lot...

"Bazil Osgood!" I exclaimed when I saw him... "You haven't changed a bit!" I exclaimed as I pulled him into a hug...

"Hello Sterling..." Bazil said as he sat down...

"Why the long face? Waitress – bring us some Hennessey!"

"I'll be right with you..." the waitress acknowledged...

"What can I do for you Sterling?"

"I'm getting married..."

"Congratulations!"

"Bazil – I have a problem..."

"I knew it!"

"Here's your drinks – what can I get you to eat?" the waitress asked as she put the drinks on the table...

"Burgers and fries..." Bazil answered...

"I'll be back..." the waitress said as she left to place our order... "Okay Sterling – what's wrong?"

"One of my clients asked me to marry her – and I said yes..."

"Sterling! You're still a Thirst Quencher?"

"Yea..."

"Sterling – what's the number one rule of Thirst Quenchers?"

"I know, I know..."

"What is it?"

"You don't fall for your clients..." I sighed...

"She knows you're an escort?"

"Yea..."

"Well I'm glad you're getting married – you're too old for that anyway – you should 'a stopped that a long time ago..."

"Here's your burgers – and here's some water..." the waitress said as she put the food and the water on the table... "Let me know if you need anything else..." she said before walking away...

"Bazil... I haven't stopped..."

"What?! Why?!"

"You know I never wanted to get married..."

"I remember..."

"Well... Lexi said I can keep my job..."

"Are you crazy?!"

"Bazil! I told her once I get married I only want to be with my wife!"

"Oh thank God!"

"But I have another problem..."

"Oh God – what?"

"Last night I was talking to Lexi – and I told her when I was with LaShonda I couldn't stop thinking about her..."

"Sterling! What the hell's a matter with you?!"

"That's not all..." I sighed...

"Sterling?"

"LaShonda went to school with Lexi – she treated Lexi like shit - so Lexi wants to confront LaShonda..."

"Sterling!"

"I know, I know – I begged her not to – I told her it would ruin me..."

"Damn Sterling..."

"What should I do?"

"Pray to God your fiancée doesn't say anything to her – other than that – I don't know what to tell you..."

"As I said – I have a proposition for you..."

"I'm listening..."

"I'm going to continue to service my clients myself until I get married..."

"What's that got to do with me?"

"Well – I was thinking we could continue to run Sterling Enterprises together..."

"I don't understand..."

"We could hire Thirst Quenchers to work for us – we take a percentage of what they earn..."

"Stop..."

"Bazil – let me finish..."

"I don't want any part of that – and neither should you..."

"What else am I supposed to do? Get a 9 to 5? Be more like you?"

"You could start your own business – something besides an escort business..."

"You used to be a Thirst Quencher too..."

"I still am – for my wife..."

"Does your wife know what you did for a living before you became a publisher?"

"Sterling – it was good seeing you..." Bazil said as he got up to leave...

"Bazil – sit – I didn't mean it like that..."

"I need to get home to my wife – give me a call as soon as you've set a date – my wife would love to meet your fiancée – we'll make a date to go out – I gotta run..." Bazil said and then he hurried out the door...

Chapter 5 - Lexi & LaShonda

"I can't wait for us to get married..." Lexi sighed to herself as she looked through the gowns...

"Welcome to David's Bridal – how may I help you – oh my God – Alexis – is that you?" LaShonda exclaimed...

"LaShonda! Oh my God! How are you?" Lexi asked as she gave LaShonda a fake hug...

"I'm actually doing great..."

"Is that right?"

"Oh yes – Fritz and I have been married for 5 years now..."

"Fritz? From high school?"

"Yes girl – he's an executive at IBM..."

"Girl! You hit the jackpot! I'm so happy for you!"

"I sure did honey – so are you looking at dresses for yourself or are you meeting someone?"

"I'm here for myself..."

"Congratulations! Le'me see your ring!"

"I don't have one yet..." Lexi laughed...

"Don't you think you should wait until you get a ring before you start looking at dresses?"

"He's not the one that proposed – I am..."

"Oh... I see..."

"What's that supposed to mean?"

"Nothing – let me look at you..." she said as she took Lexi by the hand and spun her around...

"Wow!" Lexi laughed...

"Sorry about that – I just wanted to get a look at your shape we have a spaghetti strap beaded mini dress with fringe that would look great on you..." she said as she took Lexi by the hand and led her over to the new arrivals...

"LaShonda – I don't want a mini dress – I'm getting married – I'm not going dancing..."

"You'll be dancing at your reception – and you'll be dancing on your honeymoon – you're going to need another outfit..."

"I don't think I want that LaShonda..."

"Please?"

"Well..."

"Just try it on – if you don't like it – don't take it – if you do like it – we can go back and look at some more..."

"Okay..." Lexi sighed...

"Great! You're about a size 8 – right?"

"Oh you're good..."

"Here – go try this on – hurry up – I'm so excited!"

"Okay, okay!" Lexi laughed as she took the dress and went into the dressing room...

"How's it going?"

"I'll be right out..." Lexi said as she came out and looked in the mirror...

"Oh my God – gimmie your phone!"

"Here!" Lexi laughed as she handed her phone to LaShonda... "LaShonda?"

"Yes?"

"Are you going to take the picture?"

"Oh – yes – sorry..." she said as she took a few pictures and then she gave Lexi back her phone...

"I didn't like the dress on the hanger – but now that I'm wearing it... I can't wait for Sterling to help me out of it..." Lexi sighed...

"Sterling? Is that the man on your wallpaper?"

"Yes..."

"When did you propose?"

"Last night..."

"And he said yes?"

"He sure did..." Lexi sighed...

"Congratulations – I hope you're happy..." LaShonda sighed...

"Oh I am – and I'm taking this dress too – I'll be back to look at wedding dresses later this week – thank you LaShonda..."

"You're welcome – I'll get it bagged for you..." LaShonda said as Lexi went inside the dressing room...

"Thanks again..." Lexi said as she handed LaShonda the dress...

"You're welcome – I'm going to put it in a garment bag – it will protect it and keep it from prying eyes...

"Prying eyes?"

"You don't want Sterling to see it before the big day..."

"Oh – I didn't think of that..." Lexi laughed as she deliberately handed LaShonda Sterling's Black American Express...

"Sterling Enterprises?"

"Oh shoot – I didn't mean to give you that – here – take this one..." Lexi said as she put another card on the counter and took Sterling's card back...

"May I ask what fiancé does for a living?"

"He's a personal masseuse..."

"A personal masseuse?"

"Yes..."

"You don't have a problem with that?"

"Not at all..."

"What if the women want more than a massage?"

"Oh I don't have to worry about that..."

"Good for you Lexi..."

"LaShonda – let's exchange numbers – I'd love for us to get together..."

"Oh shoot – I gotta go – there's my next appointment – hello Mrs. Johnson – how are you?" LaShonda called out as she hurried to the front of the store and Lexi left...

Chapter 6 - Shelby

"Okay Shelby – I'm here..." I said out loud as I parked the car. Shelby lived on East 95th Street off Lexington Avenue. She had a 5-bedroom, 4-bath, 3-story coop so whenever I go to visit her, we always choose a different room. She rarely tipped but I wasn't there for a tip – I was there to give her what her husband couldn't – Black Dick. Her husband was good in bed – great according to Shelby – but whenever these women talked about how good their husbands were in bed, I'd change their mind by fucking them any way they pleased, as long as they pleased, in as many positions as they pleased...

"Excuse me – may I help you?"

"Mr. Badeaux – right?" I asked as I extended my hand...

"Oh – sorry – you're here to see Mrs. Bain..."

"Yes..."

"Go ahead – she's expecting you..."

"Thank you..." I said as I went to the elevator. I couldn't stand that mutha fucka – but

I was at work – and today was payday – so I had to be nice...

"There you are!" she squealed when she saw me. I took my time going down the hall to her as I began smiling mischievously. As I walked towards her I wondered what her husband would do to her if he found out she had my dick in her mouth once a week... and I laughed to myself... "Is that smile because you're happy to see me?" she asked as she pulled me into a kiss...

"Let's go inside – you don't want your neighbors to notice...

"You don't have to worry about that – the only one home is Mr. Barreau – and he's legally blind so he wouldn't know who you were if anybody asked..." she said as she pulled me in the door, pushed me back against it, and kissed me hard...

"Did you miss me?" I breathed...

"Yes... my Thirst Quencher..." she breathed as I began kissing her on her neck... "Oh yes... don't stop..."

"Tell me what you want..." I whispered in her ear. Shelby didn't answer me – she just began unbuttoning her blouse slowly as I watched and when she was done, I walked over to her and took her breasts in my hands and massaged them...

"Oh... Yesss...." she moaned. Shelby was one of those women that are easily aroused and orgasmic when it came to touching their breasts so I did what I knew she wanted and I began alternating between licking and sucking her nipples... "Ooohhh... Yessss... Don't stop... Huh..." I stopped suddenly and she began to pout... "Why'd you stop?" I didn't answer her – I picked her up in my arms, carried her into the first bedroom, lay her on the bed, climbed up on the bed, spread her legs, and kneeled... "My Thirst Quencher... please... don't make me wait..." she begged. I took my time unbuttoning my shirt and removing it as she started breathing hard...

"Unbuckle my belt..." I commanded...

"Yes my Thirst Quencher..." she breathed as she sat up, grabbed my buckle, loosened it, and moved my pants down off my ass... "Suck my dick..." I commanded. I could never understand how a Black man could choose to be with a White woman. Don't get me wrong – it's not that I don't find them attractive – but to me – they pale in comparison to our beautiful Black women. Whenever Shelby or Samantha sucked my dick, I'd close my eyes and picture Lexi – and if I thought I was getting ready to nut too soon, I'd open my eyes and look down at them so I wouldn't...

"You like that my Thirst Quencher?" she asked as she looked up at me...

"Yeesss...." I lied. I didn't hate it – but I was at work – and today was payday – so I had to turn it up a notch... "Suck it!" I growled as I grabbed the back of her head with both hands and pushed my dick in her mouth further...

"Mmmmm..... Mmmmm..... Mmmmm....." she moaned on my dick...

"Lay back..." I commanded...

"Yes my Thirst Quencher..." she panted as she did as she was told. I looked down at her before I lay down on top of her, took her breasts in my hands, and began sucking and squeezing them... "Oh God! Yes! That feels so good!" I increased the intensity and her body began to stiffen and tremble... "I'm cumming! I'm cumming! I'm cumming!" I continued licking and sucking her breasts and nipples as her orgasm subsided and she held me against her...

"What else can I do for you?" I breathed...

"Make love to me... my Thirst Quencher..."

"As you wish..." I breathed as I got up on my knees, put the condom on, and pulled her up onto my dick by her hips...

"Oh yes... that's it..." I held her up by her hips and made love to her – if you can call it that. I could never get rough with Shelby – she couldn't handle it like LaShonda – plus – White women were quick to holler rape so I'd never put myself in that predicament... "Yes – fuck me with that Black Dick my Thirst Quencher!" she moaned...

"Is this what you want?" I growled as I fucked her deeper...

"Oh God – Yes my Thirst Quencher – Fuck me – I'm cumming!"

"Cum for me!" I commanded...

"Aaah... Aaah... Aaah... Aaah... Aaaahhhh!"

"Uuugh! Uuugh! Uuugh! Uuugh! Uuuggghhh!" I didn't pull out of Shelby right away – I stayed inside her until she stopped meeting my thrusts and then I pulled out, took off the condom, lay down, pulled her down beside me, and kissed her...

"I think I'm falling in love with you..." she breathed...

"I love you too..." I lied...

"I bet you say that to all your clients..."

"No... I don't..."

"Really?" she perked as she sat up...

"Really..." I said as I pulled her back down beside me. I was actually telling the truth – I only said that to her and Lexi...

"Could you do something else for me... my Thirst Quencher?"

"What can I do for you?"

"Well... never mind..."

"Please... let me please you... tell me..."

"I want... oral..." she sighed...

"Have you ever had your pussy eaten before?" I asked as I propped myself up on my elbow...

"No..."

"Not even by your husband?"

"He won't do it..."

"Have you asked him?"

"No..."

"Why?"

"When we were dating I brought it up – he thinks it's disgusting..." she sighed...

"Shelby... look at me..."

"I can't..." she said as she turned her head away from me...

"Please – look at me..." Shelby looked at me and I took her face in my hands and kissed her... "Who am I?"

"My Thirst Quencher..."

"Tell me what you want..."

"I want... oral..."

"Tell me what you want..."

"I want you to..."

"Say it..." I commanded as I pushed her down on her back and began kissing her down her stomach...

"My Thirst Quencher..." she moaned as she grabbed my head with her hands and began pushing me towards her pussy...

"Say it..." I breathed as I kissed the top of her pussy...

"Suck it..." she moaned...

"Suck what?" I breathed as I pulled the dental dam out my pocket and spread her lips...

"Suck my pussy!" she moaned as she arched her back, came up off the bed, and I dove in...

"OH GOD!! YES!! MY THIRST QUENCHER!!" I pulled her to me by her legs, propped myself up, and went in...

"DON'T STOP!! I'M CUMMING!! AAAGGGHHH!!" I slowed down but I didn't stop. I had a job to do – and I was going to make her first time special, unforgettable, and profitable... "AAGH... AAGH... AAGH..." she moaned as she played in my hair. I put two fingers inside her pussy, massaged her G-spot, stuck my thumb in her ass, and began sucking her clit hard... "AAAAGGGGHHHH!! MY THIRST QUENCHER!!" she screamed as she rose up off the bed, grabbed my head, and fucked my face until her orgasm subsided. I took my fingers out her pussy, my thumb out her ass, and I continued licking her clit for a few moments. When I was done, I put the dental dam in my pocket, came up between Shelby's legs, and she started to cry...

"Did I hurt you?"

"No... my Thirst Quencher..." she breathed as she pulled me into a kiss... "That was beautiful..."

"I'm glad you're pleased..."

"I think I kept you past time..."

"That's okay..."

"I'll pay you for your time..."

"Thank you..." I said as I got up, went to the bathroom, and flushed the condom and the dental dam down the toilet. When I went back into the bedroom, I picked up my shirt, put it on, buttoned it, and put on my jacket...

"I wish you didn't have to go..." she said as she got up and put on her robe...

"Same time next week?" I asked as I pulled her into a kiss...

"Same time next week..." she breathed...

"Have a good day..." I said as I left...

Chapter 7 - LaShonda

"Thank you LaShonda..." Mrs. Johnson said as LaShonda handed her the bags...

"You're welcome – enjoy your wedding..."

"I will..." Mrs. Johnson said as she left...

"Fuckin' Bitch! How the hell she pull him anyway? Bitch wasn't shit in high school and she still ain't shit – she probably ain't even gettin' married – he didn't even propose to her ass – my husband chose me – he proposed to me – he bought me my ring – she probably gonna end up buying her own ring too – I don't give a fuck – I'ma keep getting' that dick as long as I want it – matter-of-fact – I'ma tell that mutha fucka he's gonna keep giving me that dick – for free – and if he's not willing – I'll tell his stupid lil' Bitch and fuck his whole game up! Aaah Haah!" she laughed out loud as she picked up the phone...

"This is Lexi..."

"Hey Lexi – this is LaShonda..."

"How'd you get my number?"

"You wrote it on the card you filled out..."

"Oh yea – I forgot..."

"Anyway – I was calling because you said you wanted to get together..."

"Really?"

"Yes – I'd love to meet your fiancé..."

"Oh that's great!"

"Why don't we set something up for this Saturday?"

"I'd love to – I'll talk to Sterling and I'll get back to you..."

"Okay Lexi – I'll wait 'till I hear from you..."

"Okay LaShonda – bye..."

"Bye..."

"Oh this is gonna be good..." Lexi laughed...

"Stupid Bitch..." LaShonda laughed...

Chapter 8 - Sterling & Lexi

"Hey..." I said as I came in...

"Sterling – we need to talk..."

"Get your bag – we'll talk in the car..."

"Where are we going?"

"Does it matter?"

"No..."

"Okay then..." Lexi hurried about, touching up her make-up, fixing her hair, adjusting her clothes, etc... "Lexi?"

"Yes Sterling?"

"Come here..." Lexi came over to me and looked up at me. She was so beautiful. I loved the way she stood there looking at me so lovingly... "I love you..." I breathed as I pulled her into a kiss and held her...

"I love you too..."

"C'mon – let's go..." I said as I took her by the hand and led her out the door...

"Sterling – we need to talk..."

"You still wanna get married?"

"Yessss...."

"Okay then..." I said as I took her hand in mine and started the car. Lexi didn't say anything as we rode. I looked over at her a few times and each time I looked at her, she smiled back at me...

"Hmmm..." she said as I pulled into the Trumbull mall and parked near the Cheesecake Factory...

"We're here..." I said as I turned the car off, opened the door, and got out. I went around to the passenger side, opened the door before Lexi could say anything, and pulled her up into my arms...

"Sterling..." she breathed as I kissed her. I put her down, closed the door, and took her hand...

"C'mon..." I said as I led her into the mall past the Cheesecake Factory and straight to Kay Jewelers...

"Oh Sterling!" she squealed...

"Welcome to Kay Jewelers – I'm Winston – how may I help you today?"

"Hello Winston – I'm Sterling – this is Lexi – Lexi proposed... and I said yes..."

"Congratulations!"

"Thank you..." Lexi gushed...

"I never had a man come in here and tell me his lady proposed to him – you're a lucky man – maybe one day a beautiful woman will propose to me..."

"Maybe..." I agreed...

"Let me show you what we have..." Winston said as we followed him over to the show case...

"I want this one!" Lexi squealed...

"Aaahh... you like rose gold I see..."

"She loves it..." I laughed...

"Sterling – how'd you know?" Lexi asked...

"You left your laptop open... I saw your searches..."

"I can give you a great deal on this set – we also have a matching band for your future husband..."

"I know..." Lexi and I both said in unison...

"We've been trying to sell this set for a while – it's the last one we have in stock..."

"We'll take it..." I said...

"Don't you want to try it on first?" Winston laughed...

"Of course..." I laughed...

"Let's try yours on first!" Lexi exclaimed...

"That ring is a size 12 – what size are you?" Winston asked...

"It might fit..." I answered as Winston took the right out the case and Lexi took it before I could...

"Sterling – will you marry me?" she asked as she took the ring and put it on my finger as all the associates watched...

"Yes Lexi – I'll marry you..." I breathed as I kissed her and a crowd erupted in applause...

"Woo hoo!"

"Congratulations!"

"Whistle!"

"Yea!"

"Let's see if your rings fit..." I said...

"They're a size 7..." Winston said as he took them out the case...

"Lexi..." I breathed as I took the engagement ring from him and placed it on her finger... "Will you marry me?"

"Yes Sterling – yes!" she breathed as she started to cry and I pulled her into a kiss...

"Here – try on the wedding bad with it so we can make sure they both fit..." Winston said...

"I don't want to take it off..."

"You don't have to - just put the band on so I can make sure we don't have to re-size it..."

"Okay!" Lexi squealed as I put the ring on her finger...

"Okay – hold your hands like that and give me your phone – never mind – I'll use my phone..." Winston said as he went to the back. When he came back, I took my ring off and gave it to him...

"I don't want to take it off..."Lexi said...

"Just give me the band – I won't make you take off your engagement right..." Winston laughed...

"Okay..." Lexi sighed as she took off the wending band and gave it to him...

"Thank you both – do you have an account with us?"

"No..." I answered...

"I'll get you an application..." he said as he started to walk away from the counter...

"I don't want an account – I'll use my credit card..." I said as Winston ignored me and went to get an application. When he came back he put the application in front of me...

"Just sign here and give me your driver's license – I'll fill in the rest..."

"Winston – I don't want an account..."

"Yes you do..."

"Winston..."

"Sterling – let me explain to you why you need this card..."

"Okay..." I sighed...

"Once your application is approved – you get 25 percent off for opening an account – and you'll also get $50 off for every $500 you spend..."

"Okay..."

"You can pay the balance off in six months with no interest if you like..."

"Plus it helps with your commission..."

"I don't get commissions or incentives for opening accounts..."

"You don't?"

"No – I get commissions and incentives on sales..." he smiled...

"I see..." I laughed...

"I can't wait – I see a few pieces I want..." Lexi sighed. Winston and I looked at each other and smiled as I gave him my driver's license and then he took it to process the application...

"Mr. Auclair – you've been approved – your credit line is..."

"Thank you Winston..." I deliberately interrupted...

"You're welcome – would you like me to add your fiancée's name to the account?"

"No..."

"Are you sure?" he asked as Lexi looked at me and then she look at Winston...

"I'll come back and add my wife to the account after we're married..." I answered as I took Lexi by the hand and we walked over to the Cheesecake Factory...

Chapter 9 - Winston

"This is Gene..."

"Hey Gene – it's Winston from Trumbull..."

"We have a problem?"

"No Gene – but I need a favor..."

"Okay..."

"We had a couple that came in here today..."

"Let me stop you right there..."

"Gene – please..."

"Okay – go ahead..."

"She asked him to marry her – and he said yes..."

"Oh wow..."

"They bought the rose gold set..."

"No kidding! I thought we'd never sell that!"

"Never say never..." Winston laughed...

"Okay Winston – I'll review the surveillance later tonight – and I'll send you a copy so you can send it to them..."

"Thank you Gene – Sterling will be so happy when he gets it..."

"Sterling? Sterling Auclair?"

"You know him?"

"He's a nice guy..."

"Yes he is..."

"Did you get him to open an account?"

"This is Winston you're talking to..."

"My bad – how much?"

"$10,000..."

"Nice..."

"I can't wait for Lexi to come back and spend money..." Winston laughed...

Chapter 10 - Sterling & Lexi

"Welcome to the Cheesecake Factory – table for two?" the hostess asked...

"Yes – table for two..." I answered as I pulled Lexi under my arm...

"The wait will be about 25 minutes – unless you'll take outside seating..."

"We'll take outside seating!" Lexi squealed...

'Okay – follow me..." the hostess said as she brought us to the front of the restaurant facing the lobby of the mall...

"Are you sure about this Lexi?"

"Yes – I need to talk to you..."

"Okay – we'll sit here..." I said as I pulled out a chair for Lexi and she sat down...

"Your waitress will be right with you..." the hostess said as she put the menus on the table and walked away...

"Okay Lexi – what's going on?"

"Welcome to the Cheesecake Factory – my name is Michelle – I'll be taking care of you – may I start you off with something to drink?"

"I'll have a margarita..." Lexi said...

"Will that be the regular or the ultimate?"

"Regular is fine..."

"And you?"

"I'll have the El Diablo..."

"I'll be right back..." she said as she went to get our drinks...

"So... I need to tell you something..." Lexi said...

"Wait 'till we get our drinks..."

"Okay..."

"Here you are – may I take your order?" Michelle asked...

"I'll have the pasta bolognese..." Lexi answered...

"I'll have the same..."

"Okay – I'll be right back..." Michelle said a she left to place our order...

"Here's to us..." I said as I raised my glass...

"To us..." Lexi repeated as we both sipped... "I wish we could go back home and make love..." she sighed....

"I wish we could too... but..."

"You have an appointment..." Lexi sighed...

"I'm sorry..."

"I can't wait to get married..."

"Neither can I..."

"Sterling – I can't do it..."

"Do what?"

"I know I said you could keep your job... but..."

"Lexi – it'll be over soon – I promise..." I said as I took her hand...

"Are you sure? I know I said..." I didn't let her finish – I took her face in my hands and kissed her hard...

"Excuse me..." Michelle interrupted...

"Sorry about that..." Lexi laughed...

"Don't ever apologize for your fine man..." she said as she put the food on the table...

"Thank you..." Lexi blushed...

"You're welcome – I love your ring..."

"I just got it today..."

"Oh my God! Congratulations!" she exclaimed as she pulled Lacey up from the table into a hug... "I'm sorry – I'm just happy – can I get you some bread?"

"Yes – thank you..." I said...

"I'll be right back..." she said as she went to get the bread...

"Sterling – I need to tell you something..."

"Okay..."

"I went to David's Bridal yesterday..."

"Did you find a dress?"

"Here's your bread – let me know if you need anything else..." Michelle said as she placed the bread on the table and then she went to help another table...

"I found a dress... but..."

"Lexi – what's wrong?"

"LaShonda was there..."

"Lexi..."

"I didn't know she worked there – I swear – but..."

"Lexi – please – don't tell me..."

"I didn't..."

"Oh thank God..."

"She helped me pick out this dress – I told her I didn't want it but she said I'll need a dress to change into for my reception or to wear on our honeymoon... so... I bought it..."

"Why did you buy it if you don't really like it?"

"I like it – but I'm going to marry you in something else..."

"Lexi – what aren't you telling me?"

"Well... she went on and on about how well she was doing with Fritz and..."

"Fritz? Aaah Haah!"

"You're not mad?"

"Poor man hasn't got a clue..." I laughed...

"She asked me where my ring was and I told her I didn't have one yet – so she said don't you think you should wait until you get a ring before you start looking at dresses – so I told her I didn't have one yet because I proposed to you..."

"Well we took care of that – didn't we?"

"Yes we did..." Lexi sighed...

"The next time you go back to David's Bridal – you can show her..."

"I told her we should get together..."

"Lexi!"

"I know – I can't help it – I want her to know you're mine!"

"What did she say?"

"She didn't answer me yesterday – but she called me today..."

"Really?"

"She wants to get together on Saturday – I told her I'd talk to you and get back to her..."

"Oh this will be good – I haven't seen Fritz in years..." I laughed...

"What's so funny?"

"You'll see when you meet him..."

"What's he like?"

"He's like Steve Urkel..."

"No!"

"Well – not quite – but let's just say LaShonda didn't marry him for him..."

"She kept bragging about how he's an executive at IBM..."

"Lexi – back in high school – Fritz was the only guy that paid her any real attention..."

"Oh my God – and she has the nerve to be a fuckin' snob!"

"Exactly – she hasn't changed – I feel sorry for Fritz..."

"So do I..."

"Hopefully I won't have to see her anymore after Saturday – until we get married – we'll invite them to the wedding..."

"Really?"

"Absolutely – you said you wanted her to know I was yours – right?"

"Absolutely..." she breathed as she pulled me into a kiss... "I have a confession to make..."

"Yes Lexi?"

"When she took the picture of me in the dress – she used my phone..."

"And you have me as your wallpaper..."

"She asked me what you did for a living..."

"What'd you tell her?"

"I told her you were a personal masseuse – and guess what?"

"What?"

"She asked me if I was worried about other women wanting more than a massage!" Lexi laughed...

"Oh shit – now I really can't wait until Saturday!" I laughed...

"Me either!" Lexi laughed...

"I have a confession to make too..."

"Oh no – you're not cheating on me – are you?" Lexi mocked as we both laughed...

"Lexi – I'm serious..."

"Okay..."

"I had an appointment earlier today in New York..."

"Okay..."

"She told me she was falling in love with me..."

"Oh Sterling..."

"I told her I love her too..."

"Did you mean it?"

"No..."

"Does she know that?"

"Lexi – she's married – she love's Black Dick but no way in hell she's leaving her husband for it..."

"She's White?"

"Does that surprise you?"

"Yea..."

"Why?"

"I dunno – I just thought..."

"You thought I only serviced Black Women?"

"Yea..."

"It'll be over soon..."

"I can't wait..."

"Neither can I..."

"How was everything?" Michelle asked as she came over to the table...

"Everything was great..." I answered...

"Here's your check..." she said as she put it on the table...

"Here..." I said as I placed my card in the bill holder and handed it to her...

"I'll be right back..." she said as she picked up the bill and went to process it...

"I'm glad you're not mad at me..." Lexi sighed...

"For what? You didn't plan it – right?"

"No..."

"I wouldn't be mad at you if you did..."

"Here's your card – you can just sign it and leave my copy on the table..."

"Okay – thank you Michelle..."

"You're welcome – have a good day..." she said as I signed the receipt, we got up from the table, and I took Lexi's hand and walked her out the mall into the parking lot...

Chapter 11 - Samantha

"I thought you'd never get here..." she breathed as she dropped down on her knees, loosened my belt, unzipped my pants, pulled my dick out, and swallowed it...

"Oh damn..." I moaned as I grabbed her hair and pushed my dick in her mouth further....

"Mmmm... you like that my Thirst Quencher?"

"Yeess...." I breathed – and this time – I meant it... "Okay – let's go..." she commanded as she got up and led me to the bedroom by my dick...

"Yes Maam..." I said as she tugged at my dick. When we got in the bedroom she didn't waste any time – she got on the bed, lay on her back, and held her legs up... "You missed me..." I teased as I got on the bed, put on the condom, and stroked my dick...

"Oh just fuck me already!" she pleaded...

"Uh uh uh... that's not nice..."

"My Thirst Quencher... Please... I'm sorry..."

"That's more like it..." I said as I eased myself inside her slowly...

"Please my Thirst Quencher... Give it to me..."

"As you wish..." I breathed as I held her legs up by her ankles and slammed my dick inside her...

"Oh God! Yes! Fuck me!" I held on to her ankles and continued slamming my dick inside her, making sure to tilt her up just a little... "Yes my Thirst Quencher! Just like that! Don't stop! I'm cumming! Aaaaggghhh!" I smiled to myself and wondered if her neighbors heard her screaming as I kept a steady pace until she stopped me... "My Thirst Quencher..."

"Yeess..."

"Stop..."

"Is that what you want?"

"Yes..."

"Okay..." I said as I pulled out of her and let go of her legs... "Something wrong?"

"Hell no – I'll be right back..." she said as she jumped up and ran to the bathroom. I heard her flush the toilet and then she came back in the room, got on the bed on all fours, and tooted her ass towards my dick... and I knew what she wanted so I grabbed her by her hips, thrust myself inside her, and gave it to her... "Yes my Thirst Quencher... Huh... Fuck..." she moaned as I threw her back on my dick...

"You want this dick?" I growled...

"Yes my Thirst Quencher... Yes... Fuck me..." I began slapping her ass as she threw her ass back on my dick so hard I had to steady myself... "Oh God... My Thirst Quencher... Don't stop... I'm cumming!" I grabbed her hair and pulled it as I slammed my dick in her hard... "Yeesss! Aaagghhhh!"

"That's it Samantha – cum for your Thirst Quencher!" I growled...

"Aaaagggghhhh!!!"

"Yes... That's it... Like that..." I breathed as I continued pulling her hair while slowing down...

"Don't stop my Thirst Quencher..." she moaned...

"I won't stop until you want me to..."

"Oh God – I'm cumming again... Haah... Haah... Haah... Aaagghhh!" I continued thrusting until her body stopped trembling, making sure she rode out her orgasm, and then I pulled out of her...

"Get on your back..." I commanded...

"Yes my Thirst Quencher..." she breathed as she got on her back and spread her legs...

"Yeesss..." I breathed as I eased myself inside her...

"Cum for me my Thirst Quencher..." she breathed...

"As you wish..." I growled as I started fucking her harder – good thing she told me to cum when she did because between her suckin' my dick and throwin' her ass back on my like she did I was done... "Uugh! Uugh! Uugh! Uugh! Uuuggghhh!!!"

"You're welcome..." she said as she held me...

"Huh?"

"You needed that..."

"Yes... I did..."

"Thank you for waiting to give it to me..."

"How'd you know I waited?"

"I can always tell..."

"Is that right?" I asked as I pulled out of her, pulled off the condom, and propped myself up on my elbow...

"Absolutely..."

"How can you tell?"

"A man fucks different when he's pent-up..."

"Is that a good thing?"

"It's a great thing – the more pent-up you are – the better the dick you give..."

"Are you pleased?"

"Oh yea..."

"Is there anything else I can do for you?"

"I'd ask you to marry me but I'm already married..."

"That's sweet of you to say..." I said as I got up and went to the bathroom. After I flushed the condom down the toilet I went back in the room and started getting dressed...

"Same time next week?"

"Same time next week..." I breathed as I bent down and kissed her...

"Thank you..."

"You're welcome..." I said as I left...

Chapter 12 - Sterling & Lexi

"This is LaShonda..."

"Hi LaShonda – its Lexi..."

"Alexis! How are you?"

"I'm good – I'll get to the point – I spoke to Sterling and he's fine with Saturday..."

"That's great! I can't wait to see you!"

"Where shall we meet you?"

"How 'bout Bridge House in Milford?"

"I love that place..."

"Me too! Is 6:00 good?"

"Sure - will your husband be there?"

"Absolutely!"

"Good..."

"Okay Alexis – see you Saturday..."

"Lexi..."

"Okay Lexi – see you Saturday..."

"Hey..." Lexi breathed as I came in...

"Hey..." I didn't look at Lexi – I just headed for the bathroom...

"Sterling!"

"Yes Lexi?"

"I don't get a kiss hello?"

"I'm sorry – I need to get in the shower..." I answered as I went into the bathroom and closed the door... "Lexi..." I said as she pulled the glass door open and stepped in the shower with me...

"Yes Sterling?" she breathed as she pulled me into a kiss. I pulled her close to me and we held each other as we continued kissing and the water beat down on us...

"I need to take a shower..."

"We can take one together..." I couldn't argue with her. I didn't want her to leave. I was feeling guilty after leaving Samantha and I needed Lexi to make it all better... "I missed you..."

"I missed you too..." I breathed as I kissed her. My dick got hard and Lexi began stroking it.... "Lexi... wait..."

"No..." she giggled as she laid her head on my chest and continued stroking my dick..."

"Lexi – let me take a shower first..."

"Okay..." she sighed as she took the bar of soap and began washing me. I didn't stop her. I closed my eyes and enjoyed her. When she was done, she rinsed me off... "Open your eyes..." I opened my eyes, took the bar of soap, and began washing her body...

"Ooohh... Sterling..." she moaned as I went over her breasts. I continued to go over her body with the soap while kissing her down her stomach... "Ooohhh... Sterling..." she moaned again. I dropped down in front of her pussy and ran the soap across her pussy and between her legs... "Sterling..." she moaned as she grabbed my head and pushed her pussy to my face. I dropped the soap, rinsed her off, spread her lips, and dove in... "Sterling! Haah!" This wasn't the first time I ate her pussy – but it was the first time I was tasting her – and I was enjoying it... "Sterling! Don't stop! I'm cumming! I'm cumming! I'm cumming!" Lexi drenched my mouth and my face before I got up and pulled her into a kiss... "Mmmm...." she moaned in my mouth...

"Let's go to bed..."

"Okay..." she said as I took her hand and led her out the shower and into the bedroom. I picked her up in my arms, carried her over to the bed, lay her down, climbed on top of her, and spread her legs...

"Sterling..." she moaned as I eased myself inside her. Lexi always felt good but this time was different – she was the love of my life – and I wanted her... "Sterling..." she moaned...

"Lexi..." I breathed in her ear as I held her. Lexi moved her hands down my back to my ass and pushed me in deeper...

"Harder..." she moaned...

"As you wish..." I growled as I began fucking her harder...

"Oh yes... Sterling... Fuck me... Don't stop..."

"I won't Lexi... I won't..."

"Sterling! Fuck me! I'm cumming!"

"Cum for me!"

"Aaah...Aaah... Aaah... Aaah... Aaaaggghhhh!"

"Lexi... Lexi... Uggh! Uggh! Uuuuggghhhh!"

"Oh Sterling..." she breathed...

"Lexi..." I breathed as I kissed her...

"I love you so much..."

"I love you too..."

"I can't wait for this to be over..."

"It'll be over soon... I promise..."

"When?"

"When what?"

"When will this be over?" she sighed...

"Lexi – we need to talk..." I sighed as I got up...

"Sterling – come back to bed..."

"We need to talk Lexi..."

"Okay..." she sighed as she got up out the bed and put on her robe and slippers...

"You hungry?"

"Yea..."

"Come in the kitchen with me – I'll make us something to eat..." I said as I got up, put on my robe and slippers and Lexi followed me into the kitchen... "I'll make us some shrimp and pasta..." I said as I took the shrimp out the refrigerator, placed them in a bowl, filled it with water, and began cleaning them. Lexi sat at the table and watched me cleaning the shrimp.

When I was done cleaning them I seasoned them with the seafood seasoning I purchased from Riah Sanyar and put the bowl to the side. I took the linguini from the cabinet, filled a pot with water, put it on the stove, turned on the flame, and sat down at the table with Lexi...

"I'm sorry..." she sighed...

"You don't have to apologize – but I need you to understand something..."

"Okay..."

"When you asked me to marry you – you knew what I was and who I was..."

"I know – but..."

"Let me finish..."

"Okay..."

"I told you when I got married I would be with my wife exclusively..."

"Yes... you did..."

"I need you to trust me..."

"I do trust you – but..."

"Lexi..." I interrupted... "Now that we're engaged – you can't ask me about work when I come from appointments..."

"I can't talk to you?"

"When I come from appointments – I need you to let me take a shower first..."

"Are you mad at me because I wanted to take a shower with you?"

"Lexi..." I breathed as I got up and kissed her... "I'm not mad at you for what happened in the shower..." I breathed as I kissed her again... "I love what happened in the shower..."

"Me too..."

"I can't wait to do it again..."

"Me too..."

"I just need you to let me get my head right first..."

"Okay..." The water was boiling so I got up from the table, took the olive oil out the cabinet, poured some olive oil in the water, added the pasta, and went to sit back at the table with Lexi...

"I have six more appointments – and then it'll be over..."

"Do you have to keep the appointments?" she sighed...

"Yes..."

"Do you have to go back out tonight?"

"My next appointment isn't until Monday..."

"Okay..." Lexi sighed as I got up from the table, turned off the flame, drained the pasta, and took out the frying pan. I put the flame on low, poured some olive oil in the pan, and began cooking the shrimp... "That smells good..." Lexi sighed. After the shrimp was cooked, I poured the pasta into the frying pan, tossed it with the shrimp and seasoning, turned the flame off, covered it, and went back to sit at the table with Lexi... "I called LaShonda..."

"Okay..."

"She wants us to meet her at the Bridge House tomorrow at 6..."

"We can do that..."

"I can't wait to meet her husband..."

"This is going to be fun..." I laughed as I got up from the table and went over to the stove. I took two plates down from the cabinet, took the lid off the frying pan, put the pasta & shrimp on the plates, took two forks out the drawer, and brought the plates and forks to the table...

"Oh my God – this looks good!" Lexi exclaimed as she picked some up with her fork. I waited for her to taste it and when she did, I smiled... "Ooohhhh..."

"Good huh?"

"Yesss..."

"I'll let Riah know..."

"Who's Riah? Is she another client?"

"Riah is my friend in Facebook..."

"Facebook?"

"Facebook..."

"So you've never met her?"

"I've never met her..."

"How'd you find out about her?"

"She posted the link to her website, Bazil forwarded the link to me, I went to her website, I ordered her seasonings – I tried them – I liked them..."

"Where's she from?"

"She's from Washington..."

"Well this is really good – thank you..."

"You're welcome – I'll let her know..."

"Does she sell anything else?"

"She sells hair care products too..."

"Really?"

"Oh yea – she has her own hair care line..."

"Oh wow..."

"She's an author too..."

"Oh I definitely want to meet her – I want to read her books..."

"I'll connect you..."

"Okay..."

"I can't wait 'till tomorrow..."

"Me either – I'm gonna shove my ring in her face..."

"You won't have to..."

"I won't?"

"Trust me – LaShonda will look for it..." I laughed as I got up from the table, picked up the plates and forks, and put them in the sink. I took two champagne flutes down from the cabinet, took a bottle of champagne out the refrigerator, and walked back over to Lexi...

"Oooohhh... champagne..."

"Come with me..." I said, smiling mischievously. Lexi followed me into the bedroom, I put the glasses on the dresser, and when I popped the cork, it startled her...

"Oh!" she exclaimed. I poured us some champagne, picked up the glasses, and handed one to Lexi...

"Lexi... I love you..."

"I love you too..."

"Here's to our engagement..." I said as we toasted...

"To our engagement..." she breathed and then we both took a sip...

"Finish it..." I commanded. Lexi did as she was told and put the glass on the dresser. I finished my champagne, put the glass on the dresser, and pulled Lexi to me... "Who am I?" I whispered in her ear...

"My... my Thirst Quencher..." she breathed...

"Tell me what I can do for you..." I breathed as I pulled her into a kiss...

"Everything..."

"As you wish..." I said as I picked her up in my arms and carried her over to the bed...

Chapter 13 - Sterling & Lexi

"Sterling..."

"Lexi..." I yawned as I turned to face her and threw my arm around her...

"Your phone..."

"Yes... my phone..."

"Sterling..."

"Yes Lexi..."

"Your phone's ringing..."

"You want me to answer my phone? What time is it?"

"It's after 10..."

"Okay..." I yawned and then I pulled her into a kiss...

"Your phone..."

"You don't want me to kiss you?"

"Yes..."

"Yes... what?"

"Whatever you want..."

"Hold that thought..." I said as I picked up my phone and saw I had a missed call from Bazil...

"Do you need to call them back?"

"It's Bazil – le'me call him..." I said as I sat up and dialed his number..."

"Hello Sterling..."

"Hello Bazil – what's up?"

"Am I disturbing you?"

"No..."

"How's Lexi?"

"We're officially engaged..." I answered. I could see Lexi smiling and I began to smile...

"Congratulations – listen – can you stop by my office?"

"Sure – when?"

"How about Monday morning?"

"I have an appointment at 10 – can I come by at 11?"

"Will Beautiee be there?"

"Yes she will – why do you ask?"

"I'd like her to meet Lexi..."

"Aren't you coming to see me after your appointment?"

"Never mind – I need a favor though..."

"I'm not interested..."

"Here me out..."

"Okay – what?"

"I'll go make coffee..." Lexi sighed as she got up out of bed and went into the kitchen...

"We're meeting LaShonda tonight at Bridge House..."

"What the fuck is wrong with you?"

"Bazil!"

"I'm serious!" he said as I got up, went into the kitchen, and sat at the table...

"Lexi went to David's Bridal..."

"Okay..."

"She ran into LaShonda..." I explained as Lexi came to the table with two cups of coffee and sat down next to me...

"Ooohhh... now I get it..."

"LaShonda suggested we get together..."

"Does LaShonda know about you and Lexi?"

"She does – but she thinks Lexi doesn't know about her – and here's the kicker..."

"What?"

"She's married to Fritz..."

"Fritz? Aaaa Haaahhhh... Aaaa Haahhh!"

"Exactly!" I laughed...

"Sterling – I owe you an apology..."

"So you'll come tonight?"

"Hell yea – what time?"

"6..."

"Okay – we'll be there..."

"Thank you..."

"Oh no – thank you..."

"You're welcome..." I laughed...

"We'll see you later tonight..." Bazil said and then he hung up...

"I heard you invite Bazil and Beautiee..." Lexi said...

"I did..."

"Do you think that was a good idea?"

"I do..."

"I sure hope so..." she sighed...

"Lexi..." I said as I got up from the table and went over to her... "We're going to announce our official engagement, we're going to eat, we're going to drink, and then I'm going to bring you home and spend the rest of the night making love to you..."

"Okay..."

"Bazil and Beautiee will celebrate with us and LaShonda will have no choice but to sit through it..."

"Can I ask you something?"

"Yes Lexi?" Lexi pulled me to her, wrapped her legs around me, and wrapped her arms around my neck...

"Can we do it again?"

"Depends on what it is..." I breathed as I kissed her...

"All of it..."

"As you wish..." I breathed as I picked her up and carried her into the bedroom...

Chapter 14 – Bazil & Beautiee

"I can't wait 'till tonight..." Beautiee sighed...

"Neither can I..." Bazil breathed in her ear as he kissed her earlobe and moved down to her neck...

"Bazil..." Beautiee moaned...

"Yes Beautiee..." Bazil breathed as he kissed her down her chest and took her right nipple in his mouth...

"I... I..."

"Sssshhh..." Bazil whispered as he put his finger over her mouth... and Beautiee bust out laughing... "What's so funny?"

"You just sshheed me..." she laughed...

"You're right..." he laughed... "That is funny..."

"You know I can't be quiet..." she said as she pulled him into a kiss...

"I know..." he breathed as he kissed her back and pushed his tongue in her mouth...

"Mmmm..." she moaned as he walked her backwards towards the bed. Beautiee pulled him down on top of her, spread her legs, moved her hands down to his ass, and squeezed it as Bazil continued tonguing her down for a few moments... "Fuck me..." Beautiee breathed...

"Tell me again..." Bazil breathed a she eased himself inside her...

"Fuck me!" she moaned as he began thrusting... "Harder!" she moaned. Bazil was more than willing to oblige...

"Is this what you want?"

"Yes! Fuck me! I'm cumming! I'm cumming!"

"Cum for me!"

"Aaagh! Aaagh! Aaagh! Aaagh! Aaaaggghhhh!"

"Fuck! Uuuuggghhhh!" Beautiee pulled Bazil down and held him as her body trembled... "That's it Beautiee..." Bazil breathed as he kissed her neck and shoulder... "Give it to me..." Bazil kissed Beautiee again and she wrapped her legs around his back and locked her ankles together... "Mmmm... you want more..."

"Yeesss..."

"I love it when you want me..." he breathed as he started thrusting again...

"Bazil... Haa...."

"Fuck!" Bazil pushed his tongue in her mouth and fucked her deeper...

"Mmmm... Mmmm... Mmmm... Mmmm..."

"Mmmph! Mmmph! Mmmph! Mmmph!"

"Mmmm... Mmmm... Mmmm... Mmmm..."

"Mmmph! Mmmph! Mmmph! Mmmph!"

"Mmmm... Mmmm... Mmmm... Mmmm... Mmmmmmmm!"

"Mmmph! Mmmph! Mmmph! Mmmph! Mmmmppphhhh!" Bazil continued tonguing Beautiee down as their orgasms subsided and she unlocked her ankles and then he got up off her, lay down beside her, and propped his head up on his elbow... "We need to talk..."

"Yes my Thirst Quencher?"

"That's what I need to talk to you about..."

"Okay..."

"Sterling worked with me..."

"Really?"

"Yes..."

"Oh wow..."

"Lexi is – was – one of his clients..."

"Oh!" Beautiee exclaimed...

"She fell in love with Sterling and asked him to marry her..."

"Oh my God – that's so romantic..." Beautiee whispered as she started crying...

"Are you okay?" Bazil asked as he wiped her tears...

"I'm okay... it's just..."

"Beautiee... what's wrong?"

"I was just thinking about when you asked me to marry you..."

"I love you Beautiee..."

"I love you too..."

"We're going to dinner with them to celebrate their engagement..."

"Awww..."

"There's more..."

"Bazil... what's wrong?"

"I don't know how to tell you..." Beautiee sat up in bed and Bazil sat up next to her...

"Bazil?"

"Sigh... Lexi went to David's Bridal and ran into LaShonda..."

"Who's LaShonda?"

"LaShonda went to school with Lexi..."

"Oh that's nice – will she be there tonight?"

"Yes – and so will her husband..."

"Oh that's nice!' Beautiee exclaimed...

"Not exactly..."

"What's going on Bazil?"

"We went to school with Fritz..."

"LaShonda's husband?"

"Yes..."

"Bazil?"

"Sigh... LaShonda is one of Sterling's clients..."

"Wait... wait... wait..."

"Yes..."

"You mean to tell me – Lexi proposed to Sterling – he said yes – she goes shopping for a wedding dress – runs into LaShonda – who's also fucking her fiancé – Bazil?"

"Yes Beautiee?"

"Does LaShonda know that Lexi proposed to Sterling?"

"Yes..."

"Fuckin' Bitch!" Beautiee laughed...

"Exactly..."

"Does Lexi know LaShonda is one of Sterling's clients?"

"Yes..."

"Oh I like her already!" Beautiee exclaimed...

"You do?"

"She knows LaShonda's fuckin' her man – you both went to school with her husband – oh this is gonna be good!" Beautiee laughed...

"I'm surprised you're taking this so well..." Bazil laughed...

"Fritz has no idea – does he?"

"No..."

"Lexi's about to shut shit down!" Beautiee laughed...

"Beautiee – you can't tell her what I told you..."

"I won't..." Beautiee said as she pulled Bazil into a kiss...

Chapter 15 – Fritz & LaShonda

"Oh Shonda..." Fritz moaned as his orgasm was building...

"Not yet... almost there..." LaShonda breathed...

"Shonda... Shonda... Shondaaaa!" Fritz moaned as he came. LaShonda pushed him off her and turned her back to him... "I'm sorry..." he whispered as he reached out to touch her and she pushed his hand away...

"I'm so tired of you being sorry!" she snapped as she went to get up and Fritz pushed her back down on her back and got on top of her... "Get off me Fritz..."

"No..." he laughed as he kissed his way down her stomach...

"Fritz... stop..."

"No..." Fritz breathed as he kissed her pussy lips...

"Fritz..." Fritz ignored her as he spread her lips with his tongue and flicked her clit...

"Ooohhh..." she moaned. Fritz took that as his cue to continue so he spread her lips, took her clit in his mouth, and began sucking it hard...

"Fffrrriiitttzzzz! Oh God! Don't Stop!" Fritz stopped sucking her clit, put his tongue inside, and began tongue-fucking her as he shook his nose back and forth against her clit... "Fffrrriiitttzzz! Oh God! Don't stop!" she screamed as she grabbed his head with her hands and fucked his face... "I'm cumming! Aaaaggghhh!" Fritz flicked his tongue on her clit as her body trembled from multiple orgasms and just when she thought he was finished – he came up between her legs and thrust himself inside her... "Oh Fritz..." LaShonda moaned as he fucked her deeper...

"Yes Shonda..." Fritz breathed as she pulled him down and held him...

"Fuck... I'm cumming..." she moaned...

"Cum for me..."

"Ohh... Ohh... Ohh... Ohh... Oooohhhh!"

"Shonda... Shonda... Shonda... Shonda... Ssshhhooonnndddaaa!" Fritz collapsed on top of her and kissed her so hard it startled her...

"Damn that was good..." she breathed...

"You alright now?" Fritz breathed as he kissed her...

"Hell yea..." she breathed...

"Let's go take a shower..."

"Okay!" she squealed as she jumped up and ran towards the bathroom...

Chapter 16 – Sterling & Lexi

"Lexi... Shhiiiittt!" I moaned as she took my dick in her mouth and down her throat...

"Mmmm..." she moaned on my dick and I lost it...

"Lexi... Lexi..."

"Don't you dare..." she said after she snatched her mouth off my dick and stroked it with her hands...

"Lexi... please..."

"Ooohhh... you're begging..." she said as she put my dick back in her mouth...

"Lexi... Fuck... I can't hold it..." Lexi massaged my balls as she took my dick all the way down and I shot up off the bed... "Lllleeeexxxxiiii!! Aaaagggghhhh!" Lexi propped herself up between my legs and continued sucking and massaging my balls as she swallowed every drop... "Got damn..." I breathed as she continued sucking and massaging. This was the first time I'd actually felt Lexi's mouth on my dick without a condom... and it felt good...

"Who are you?" she asked as she stroked my dick...

"I'm your Thirst Quencher..." I breathed...

"Whose dick is this?"

"Yours Lexi..." I breathed. Lexi came up between my legs, pushed herself up on top of me, spread her legs, pushed herself onto my dick, and sat upright... "Oh shit..." I breathed as she started bouncing on my dick. I grabbed Lexi by her ass and met her every thrust...

"Fuck me..." she moaned. That did it. I flipped Lexi over on her back and began pounding her pussy... "Sterling... Sterling... Sterling..."

"Gimmie that pussy!" I growled as I continued pounding her...

"Ssstttееerrrllliiinnnggg! I'm cumming! Aaaggghhh!"

"Llleexxxiii... Llleeexxxiii... Fffuuucccckkk... Aaaggghhh!" I collapsed on top of Lexi and she began to cry... "Lexi... please... don't cry..." I said as I teared up...

"I can't help it..."

"Lexi... what's wrong?"

"This was our first time..."

"Yes... it was..." I breathed as I kissed her...

"You feel so good..."

"You feel good too..." I breathed as I kissed her again...

"Your dick felt so good in my mouth..."

"I love how you sucked my dick..."

"I can get pregnant now..."

"You might be pregnant already..." I breathed as I kissed her again...

"You sure you don't have to go out until Monday?"

"I'm sure..."

"Good..." she breathed as she put her legs up, locked her ankles behind my back, pulled me into a kiss, and we went for round two... "Mmmm... Mmmm... Mmmm... Mmmm..."

"Mmmph! Mmmph! Mmmph! Mmmph!"

"Mmmm... Mmmm... Mmmm... Mmmm..."

"Mmmph! Mmmph! Mmmph! Mmmph!"

"Mmmm... Mmmm... Mmmm... Mmmm... Mmmmmmmm!"

"Mmmph! Mmmph! Mmmph! Mmmph! Mmmmppphhhh!" I continued tonguing her down as our orgasms subsided and she unlocked her ankles and then I got up off her, lay down beside her, and propped my head up on my elbow... "Lexi... we need to talk..."

"Okay..." she sighed...

"Bazil used to work with me..."

"Really?" she asked as she sat up in bed...

"Yes..." I answered as I sat up beside her...

"Is that how he met Beautiee?"

"I don't think so..."

"How did this start?"

"What?"

"Thirst Quenchers?"

"We started in high school..."

"Oh wow!" she exclaimed...

"We could have girls anytime we wanted them and they were willing to pay us so we went with it..."

"Who came up with the name?"

"Bazil..."

"Was it just you and Bazil?"

"Naa – some of the ball players were Thirst Quenchers too..."

"Oh my God!"

"We had a plan – well – some of us had a plan..."

"A plan? What do you mean?"

"We all talked about doing what we were doing – Thirst Quenchers – until we met the love of our lives and then we'd stop..."

"So how did this work?"

"Bazil and I recruited males..."

"So you were pimps?"

"Oh no – we were always watching – we knew what guys got the pussy so we pulled them to the side and mentored them..."

"You mentored them?"

"We told them about safe sex and we told them to be selective..."

"Be selective?"

"When you're young, you think with the wrong head – you don't care where the pussy comes from as long as you get it..."

"Oh wow..."

"We wanted to make sure the boys didn't get themselves in trouble..."

"Did you ever have sex with any of the teachers?"

"Bazil didn't – but I did..."

"Really?"

"Bazil said he didn't trust any of the teachers – especially the White ones – because White women and White girls were quick to cry rape..."

"Oh my God!"

"I remember I had sex with my science teacher..."

"You did?"

"Her name was Ms. Hiduque..."

"Was she White?"

"No – she was Black..."

"So you had an affair?"

"Hell no – she bought me clothes, she gave me money, I had sex with her, and then I avoided her..."

"You avoided her?"

"Lexi – she was a teacher – I had no plans to be in a sexual ship with her – or anybody else at that time..."

"Would you have done that to me?" she asked as she turned to face me...

"Lexi... I love you... I fell in love with you..." I breathed as I kissed her...

"So if I met you in high school you would've stopped..."

"Absolutely..."

"You're still doing it though..."

"Lexi..."

"Bazil stopped... but you didn't..."

"Bazil found his first love in high school..."

"Beautiee?"

"Bazil's first love was books..."

"Books?"

"Bazil wrote his first book in high school. Bazil talked about having his own publishing company and publishing other authors so much the guys didn't want to be around him unless he was talking about pussy..." I laughed...

"They weren't really his friends..."

"They didn't have any goals beyond pussy and high school – that was another reason Bazil wouldn't have sex with teachers..."

"He was really focused..."

"Yes he was – and it paid off..."

"You still look up to him?"

"Yea..."

"Why me?"

"What are you asking me Lexi?"

"What made you say yes?"

"I love you..."

"I love you too – but that doesn't answer my question..."

"When you asked me to marry you... I knew you loved me for me..."

"Aww..."

"I didn't think I'd ever find that..." I said as I started tearing up...

"Sterling..." Lexi whispered as she pulled my face to hers and kissed my eyes and then my mouth... "When I asked you to marry me I was scared to death..."

"Lexi! Why?"

"I was afraid you'd say no..."

"I did... at first..."

"You tried to let me down gently because you didn't think I was serious..."

"Lexi..." I breathed as I pulled her into a kiss... "How'd you know that?"

"I felt it..." she breathed as the kissed me again...

Chapter 17 – Bridge House

"Welcome to Bridge House..." the hostess said as Fritz and LaShonda walked inside... "Do you have a reservation?"

"Yes we do..." Fritz answered...

"May I get your name?"

"Aubert..."

"Oh yes – table for four – right?"

"Yes – that's right..."

"All the tables for four have been reserved; however, we can seat you at a table for six on the deck if you like..."

"What's the point of making a reservation if we can't get a table?" LaShonda snapped...

"We'll take it..." Fritz said...

"I'm sorry for the mix-up – please follow me..." she said as they followed her to the table and sat down...

"Would you like me to bring you some menus while you wait?"

"Yes please..." Fritz answered...

"I'll be right back..." the hostess said as she went to get the menus...

"Shonda – let's try to have a nice evening – okay?"

"Why wouldn't I want us to have a nice evening?" LaShonda snapped...

"Shonda..." he said as he took her hand and kissed it... "Please..."

"Okay..."

"Welcome to Bridge House – do you have a reservation?"

"Hi Mr. Osgood!" somebody yelled...

"Hello..." Bazil said as he turned and smiled...

"Mr. Osgood? Oh my God – I'm so embarrassed!"

"Don't be..."

"Let me check... oh shoot – I don't see a reservation for you – I already messed up one reservation..."

"We don't have a reservation..." Bazil said...

"Oh thank God – I mean – thank God I didn't mess up another reservation – there's a 20-minute wait..."

"We're with the Auberts..." Beautiee said...

"Oh! They're expecting you – right this way..."

"We're waiting on two more..."

"Hmmm – she said the reservation was for four – good thing I seated them at a table for six..."

"That is a good thing..." Bazil said as we walked in...

"Bazil!" I exclaimed...

"Nice to see you again Sterling..." Bazil said as he got up and we embraced...

"Oh my God – le'me see!" Beautiee exclaimed as she took Lexi's hand and held it up...

"I'm Alexis – but my friends call me Lexi..."

"Hi Lexi – I'm Beautiee – and this is my husband Bazil..."

"Nice to meet you Lexi..." Bazil said...

"Nice meeting you too..." Lexi said...

"Hi – I'm Natasha..." the hostess interrupted as we all laughed...

"Nice meeting you Natasha..." Beautiee said...

"Oh my God – your ring is gorgeous – how long have you been engaged?"

"24 hours..." Lexi sighed...

"Oh my God – come with me – I need to get you seated – and I need to get a picture!" Natasha said as she grabbed six menus and utensils and then we followed her to the table on the deck...

"Bazil! Sterling! Hey!" Fritz exclaimed when he saw us. Fritz got up from the table and came over to embrace us and Natasha took the picture...

"Excuse me!" LaShonda exclaimed...

"I'm sorry – I wanted Lexi to have a couple of pictures from her engagement party..." Natasha sighed...

"Ladies – get together so Natasha can get a picture of you..." I said. It took everything in my not to bust out laughing as LaShonda forced a smile...

"C'mon ladies! This is a happy occasion! Smile!" Natasha exclaimed...

"Lexi – why don't you get in the middle so you can flash that gorgeous ring?!" Beautiee exclaimed...

"Okay!" Lexi squealed as she got in between them and Natasha took the picture...

"Thank you Natasha..." Lexi sighed...

"You're welcome – can I start you off with a bottle of champagne?"

"Fine with me!" Lexi squealed...

"Me too girl!" Beautiee laughed...

"I'll be right back!" Natasha exclaimed...

"LaShonda – thank you so much!" Lexi squealed as she pulled LaShonda into a hug...

"You're very welcome..." LaShonda lied... "Nice meeting you Bazil, Beautiee..."

"Nice meeting you too – how long have you and Lexi known each other?"

"Alexis and I went to high school together..."

"Lexi..." Lexi corrected...

"Shonda..." Fritz said...

"Shonda – I like that!" Lexi said...

"I don't..." LaShonda said...

"Shonda – you promised..." Fritz said as he took her hand and kissed it...

"Okay..." she sighed...

"We all went to school together..." Fritz said...

"Beautiee – I don't recall seeing you in high school – did you go to another school?" LaShonda asked...

"I went to school in New York..." Beautiee answered...

"I see..." LaShonda smirked...

"I fell for LaShonda as soon as I saw her..." Fritz said...

"How sweet!" Lexi exclaimed...

"I meet Beautiee at night... and I proposed to her in the morning..." Bazil said...

"Oh my God! That's so romantic!" Lexi exclaimed...

"Let me get this straight – you met Beautiee at night – and proposed the next day? And Beautiee said yes?"

"I sure did..." Beautiee sighed as she pulled Bazil into a kiss...

"You're a better woman than me..." LaShonda said...

"I'm a happy woman..." Beautiee said...

"Lexi proposed to me... and I said yes..." I said as I pulled Lexi into a kiss...

"Sterling! Congratulations!" Fritz exclaimed...

"Thank you Fritz..." I said as I looked over at LaShonda...

"Here's your champagne..." Natasha said as she came to the table with a *tray* of glasses and the bottle of champagne...

"Finally!" LaShonda snapped...

"Let me get that..." Fritz said as he picked up the bottle and popped the cork...

"Got it!" Natasha said as she took the picture. Fritz got up and poured our glasses...

"Okay everyone – take a glass!" Natasha said. We all picked up a glass as we were told... "Smile!" Natasha said as we held our glasses up... "On three – one... two..."

"Three!" we all said in unison as Natasha took the picture...

"To Sterling and Lexi!" Fritz said as he raised his glass...

"To Sterling and Lexi!" we all said in unison and then we all drank the champagne....

"Got it!" Natasha said as she took pictures...

"Can we get some appetizers?" LaShonda asked as we all sat down...

"Sure – what would you like?"

"I'll have the crisp jumbo lump crab cakes, fritto misto, and hot artichoke & spinach dip..."

"Ooohhh – that sounds good!" Lexi exclaimed...

"Sure does!" Beautiee agreed...

"I'll bring three of each – how's that?"

"That's fine Natasha..." I answered...

"I'll be back..." Natasha said as she went to place the order...

"So Beautiee – what do you do in your spare time?" LaShonda asked...

"Sleep!" Beautiee laughed...

"That busy huh?"

"Four babies... running a publishing company... writing... yea..."

"Oh so you work with your husband?"

"I do..."

"And you write too?"

"I do..."

"What's the title of your latest book?"

"In The Arms Of A Gangster..."

"Oh my God! I love that series!" Lexi exclaimed...

"You read my books?" Beautiee asked...

"Yes! I can't believe I'm sitting here with Beautiee!"

"Thank you Lexi..."

"Isn't that the book where you talk about your husband being with a man?" LaShonda asked...

"Shonda!" Fritz snapped...

"So you've read my books too?" Beautiee asked...

"I have..."

"Thank you..." Beautiee said. Bazil and I looked at Fritz and then we looked at each other. Fritz glared at LaShonda and Beautiee took the opportunity to dig in a bit... "So LaShonda – what do you do?"

"I don't have to work – my husband takes care of me..."

"Here's your appetizers..." Natasha said as she put the appetizers on the table, took a couple of pictures, and went to another table... "That's great – but that doesn't answer my question..." Lexi began to smile as LaShonda turned beat red...

"Right now I'm just enjoying my husband..." LaShonda sighed...

"Do you want children?"

"We wanted to enjoy being married for a while..." Fritz answered...

"How 'bout you Lexi?" Beautiee asked...

"We want children..." Lexi sighed as she took my hand and squeezed it...

"How's everything?" Natasha asked as she came back over to the table...

"Everything's fine..." Lexi sighed...

"Are you ready to order your main course?"

"I am..." LaShonda answered...

"What would you like?"

"I'd like the pan roasted salmon..."

'I'll have the seared scallops..." Lexi said...

"I'll have the mixed grill..." Beautiee said...

"I'll have the steak frites..." Fritz said...

"I'll have the cowboy steak..." Bazil said...

"I'll have the double cut Berkshire pork chop..." I said...

"Got it!" Natasha said as she went to place our order...

"Fritz – are you still at IBM?" Bazil asked...

"I am..."

"What do they have you doing these days?"

"I'm in corporate litigation..."

"Nice!" Bazil said...

"You've done pretty nice yourself..." Fritz said...

"Yes I have..." Bazil agreed...

"I bet you love having your wife at work with you every day..." Fritz said...

"I love working with my husband..." Beautiee sighed as she looked at Bazil...

"Don't you need space?" LaShonda asked...

"Nope..."

"I wouldn't mind working with Sterling..." Lexi sighed...

"Why don't you work with him then?" Fritz asked...

"Sterling is a personal masseuse..."

"So what?"

"I don't understand..."

"Sterling is a personal masseuse – right?"

"Yes..."

"He has clients – right?"

"Yes..."

"Each client has a significant other – you can do couple massages..."

"That's a great idea..." I said...

"I don't know how to do a personal massage..." Lexi said...

"You know how to have sex don't cha?"

"Yea... but..."

"If you can touch your husband – you can give a massage – besides – Sterling will teach you everything you need to know..."

"I never thought of that – thank you Fritz!" I exclaimed...

"You're welcome..."

"We'll be your first couple..." Bazil said...

"You will?!" I exclaimed...

"We'll talk on Monday..." Bazil answered...

"Ready for your entrees?" Natasha asked as she came to the table with our food and began placing the food on the table...

"Ooohhh – this looks good!" Lexi exclaimed...

"It does..." I agreed...

"Okay – everybody smile!" Natasha said as she took a few pictures...

"You didn't give us a chance..." LaShonda said...

"Don't worry – the pictures will be great..." Natasha said as she put her phone in her pocket and went to take care of another table...

"I can't wait to start working with you..." Lexi said...

"I can't wait to start teaching you..." I said...

"We love it..." Beautiee said...

“How do you manage to do that with four babies?” Fritz asked...

“I work from home until they can talk...”

“I see...”

“Do you ever have to bring the kids to work with you?” LaShonda asked...

“We bring the kids to work with us because we want to...” Bazil answered...

“I can put in a good word for you if you’d like to come work with me... if you want...” Fritz said as he turned to LaShonda...

“I’m enjoying being at home right now...” LaShonda said. We finished eating without speaking. Bazil and I smiled at each other as we caught glances between Beautiee and Lexi...

“How’s everything?” Natasha asked as she came back over to our table...

“Everything was good!” Lexi exclaimed...

“I’ll pass that on – can I get you anything else?”

“Check please!” LaShonda answered...

“Thank you Fritz, thank you LaShonda...” I said...

“You’re very welcome...” Fritz said as Natasha went to get our check...

“I’m so glad you got a table for six...” Lexi said...

“Me too – thank you for inviting us Sterling...” Beautiee said...

“Sterling invited you?” LaShonda asked...

"I wanted to make it special for Lexi..." I answered...

"Thank you..." Lexi sighed as she pulled me into a kiss...

"You're welcome..." I breathed as I kissed her back...

"Here's your check..." Natasha said as she took one final picture... "Congratulations Lexi – nice to see you again Mr. & Mrs. Osgood..."

"Thank you Natasha..." Lexi said as we got up...

"Come to the front and give me your phone number so I can text you the pictures..."

"Okay!" Lexi squealed...

"Do you mind if I keep a copy?"

"I don't mind – do you Beautiee?"

"I'm used to it..." Beautiee laughed... "Make sure you tag me when you post them to Facebook..."

"Yes Maam!" Natasha exclaimed...

"Well I mind!" LaShonda snapped...

"Shonda... we're out with friends celebrating their engagement – so what people will see us having a good time – what's wrong with that?" Fritz asked...

"Nothing..." LaShonda answered...

"Good! Now let's go pay this check so we can go home... and then you can give me some dessert!" he said as he slapped LaShonda on her ass...

"Fritz!" she exclaimed. Beautiee looked at Bazil, Lexi looked at me. Bazil and I looked at each other and smiled...

Chapter 18 – Sterling & Lexi

"I love you!" I yelled as I picked Lexi up and spun her around...

"I love you too!" she laughed. I pulled Lexi down to my mouth and kissed her hard. Lexi wrapped her legs around my waist and I started to carry Lexi into the bedroom but she stopped me... "Sterling... wait..."

"Why?" I asked as I put her down...

"What's this?" she asked as she picked up an envelope from Kay Jewelers...

"Maybe it's the credit card..."

"Sure is a big envelope for a credit card..." she said as she ripped it open...

"There's goes the surprise..." I laughed...

"This wasn't a surprise..."

"What makes you so sure?"

"Because you didn't try to stop me from opening it..." she said as she pulled out a letter... "Ooohhh look – it's from Winston!"

"Le'me see..." I said as I stood beside her and we both started reading...

"Dear Sterling & Lexi,

Congratulations on your engagement.

Thank you for giving me hope.

Please enjoy this.

Love,

Winston."

"Look – there's a disc in here..." Lexi said as she pulled the disc out the envelope...

"Hmmm... look..." I said as I showed the disc to Lexi...

Sterling & Lexi
Friday, March 13th, 2020

"Aww..." Lexi sighed as I put the disc in the CD player and we started watching... "The ring!"

"You look so happy..."

"Look at you!"

"I was happy too..."

"I can't believe Winston did this for us..."

"I want to invite him to the wedding..."

"Okay..."

"This is where we ask each other..." I said as I pulled Lexi to me and held her...

"I love you so much..."

"I love you too..." I breathed as I kissed her... and then she bust out laughing...

"What's so funny?"

"I think Beautiee knows..."

"You do? What makes you say that?"

"She went at LaShonda!" Lexi laughed...

"That had nothing to do with the Thirst Quenchers..." I laughed...

"Really?"

"Oh yea – Beautiee doesn't take any shit from anybody – she caught a woman trying to come on to Bazil and she threw the woman out by her hair!" I laughed...

"Oh my God! I remember reading about that in her book!"

"LaShonda's no match for her... or you..."

"Me?"

"Lexi – you're not in high school anymore – don't let LaShonda make you feel like you're beneath her..."

"I don't feel that way anymore..."

"You sure?"

"She put on a front like she was such a happy woman that had it all – the truth is she's miserable – and now that I took you away from her she'll really be miserable!" Lexi laughed...

"I guess you don't want her at the wedding..." I laughed...

"I'm not sure..."

"What do you mean?"

"I don't know if I want a big wedding..."

"I'd like to invite Bazil and Beautiee..."

"Me too..."

"But you don't want LaShonda..."

"I like Fritz... but..."

"It bothers you that I had sex with her..."

"Yea..."

"We don't have to invite them..."

"Thank you..." she said as she pulled me into a kiss..."

"You ready for dessert?"

"Yea..."

"Come with me..." I said as I took her by the hand and led her into the bedroom...

Chapter 19 – Bazil & Beautiee

"Mommy! Daddy!" Lydia squealed when she saw them...

"How's Mommy's girl?" Beautiee asked as she picked Lydia up...

"I'm bein' have – right Auntie Keisha?"

"Yes Lydia – you bein' have..." she laughed...

"Y'all have a good time?" Troy asked...

"Yea..." Beautiee sighed...

"You got pictures?" Keisha asked...

"The hostess took pictures..." Bazil answered...

"Lydia – go upstairs and play..." Keisha said...

"I want Mommy..."

"Go upstairs Lydia..." Beautiee said...

"You go bye bye Mommy?"

"No Lydia..."

"Okay – bye..." Lydia said as she ran upstairs...

"Okay Beautiee – what's wrong wichall?" Keisha asked...

"Girl – I don't even know where to start..." Beautiee sighed...

"Girl – what happened?"

"Lexi proposed to Sterling – Sterling said yes – so they got engaged yesterday..."

"You don't have any pictures?"

"She didn't post them yet..."

"Okay – so it was an engagement party?"

"Lexi & Sterling thought so..."

"Wait – what?"

"Lexi went to David's Bridal to look at wedding dresses and LaShonda was there..."

"LaShonda? I went to school with her – I can't stand her ass!"

"Me either!"

"Damn – what LaShonda do to y'all?" Troy laughed...

"We all went to high school together..." Bazil answered...

"Oh so you know her too?" Troy asked...

"Oh yea..."

"Oh God – don't tell me..." Keisha said...

"Hell no!" Beautiee laughed...

"Bazil – what the fuck they talkin' about?" Troy laughed...

"Your wife was asking Beautiee if I fucked her..." Bazil laughed...

"Yo – I can't!" Troy laughed...

"Fritz is a nice guy – LaShonda doesn't deserve him..." Beautiee said...

"I know – he tried to holla at me but I wasn't interested..." Keisha said...

"Oh shit!" Bazil exclaimed...

"Don't get me wrong – he was nice – but he's not my type..."

"I know that's right!" Troy said as he pulled Keisha into a kiss...

"When I saw Troy – I knew – when I saw Fritz – uh uh..."

"He's not LaShonda's type either..." Beautiee said...

"Beautiee – don't..." Bazil interrupted...

"It's okay – they won't tell..."

"Oh shit – you know you gotta tell me – right?" Keisha asked...

"Keisha – you know how you always tell me about Mary?"

"Oh shit – LaShonda wants Sterling!" Keisha exclaimed...

"Yes..."

"Beautiee – what makes you say that?" Troy asked...

"You and Keisha are genuinely affectionate – Bazil and I are all over each other every chance we get – Lexi and Sterling were so romantic at the restaurant – and LaShonda paid more attention to Sterling than her own husband..." Beautiee answered...

"Damn..." Troy sighed...

"He only married her 'cause she gave him some in high school..." Keisha said...

"And now that I've met her – I bet she only gave him some so he would marry her..." Beautiee laughed...

"To be honest – we weren't even invited..." Bazil said...

"Oh shit!" Troy exclaimed...

"Sterling called me and since Fritz was going to be there he thought it would be nice if we showed up..." Bazil said...

"So you like Lexi?" Keisha asked...

"Oh yea – if I knew y'all went to school together I would've invited you and Troy too..." Beautiee answered...

"Beautiee doesn't like LaShonda too much..." Bazil laughed...

"And she doesn't like me either – and I don't give a fuck!" Beautiee laughed...

"You had to check her?" Keisha asked...

"You already know!" Beautiee laughed...

"Girl – what happened?"

"She tried it – talkin' 'bout... so Beautiee – what do you do in your spare time?"

"No the fuck she didn't!"

"She did – so I told her I sleep in my spare time – she goin' ask me... that busy?"

"No she didn't!"

"So I said four babies – running a publishing company – writing – yea..."

"Damn I wish I was there!" Keisha exclaimed...

"So she asked about my books and what was the title of my latest book and when I tell her she says... isn't that the book where you write about your husband being with a man?"

"Oh hell no – you should 'a slapped that Bitch!" Keisha exclaimed...

"Beautiee thanked her for reading her books..." Bazil laughed...

"I love y'all – I sear!" Troy exclaimed...

"We love y'all too..." Bazil said...

"Fritz checked her..." Beautiee said...

"Oh shit – that's a damn shame..." Keisha said...

"If Fritz didn't take LaShonda's hand there wouldn't have been any affection at all..." Bazil said...

"You know I couldn't let her get away with that shit – right?" Beautiee laughed...

"Girl – tell me!" Keisha exclaimed...

"I asked her what she does all day and she goin' say... I don't need to work – my husband takes care of me..."

"She was just like that in high school..." Keisha said...

"I said that's nice – but that doesn't answer my question..."

"I know that's right – git that ass!" Keisha laughed...

"Fritz suggested Lexi learn to do massage so they could do couples..." Bazil said...

"I like that..." Troy said...

"Fritz told LaShonda he'd put in a good word for her if she wanted to come work with him and she told him she wants to enjoy staying home..." Bazil laughed...

"Bitch ain't worked since we left high school!" Keisha laughed...

"Well she was at David's Bridal helping Lexi pick out dresses so I guess she does something sometime..." Beautiee laughed... "I asked her if they wanted children and she goin' say... we wanted to enjoy being married for a bit first..."

"Shit – she getting' old – she better hurry up before her eggs dry up!" Keisha laughed...

"Damn Keisha – that's fucked up!" Troy laughed...

"Oh well!" Keisha laughed...

"Do you want any more children Troy?" Bazil asked...

"It ain't up to me – it's up to Keisha..."

"I said I'd think about it – don't push me..." Keisha said...

"I'm sorry – I can't help it..." Troy said...

"This your damn fault!" Keisha exclaimed...

"Me? How's it my damn fault?" Beautiee laughed...

"Troy looks at y'all and thinks it's easy..." Keisha laughed...

"Sorry – not sorry..." Beautiee laughed...

"I bet Amina would love another sister..." Bazil said...

"Sister or brother – if we have another one – we sendin' them both to your house..." Keisha laughed...

"That's fine..." Bazil said...

"I'm getting tired..." Beautiee yawned..."

"You aint' gotta stay!" Keisha laughed...

"Kids – let's go!" Bazil boomed...

"Coming Daddy!" they all said in unison and then they came charging downstairs...

"Amina – where you goin'?" Troy asked...

"I'm goin' with them!" Amina beamed...

"It's fine – c'mon..." Beautiee said as she got up to leave and Bazil and the kids followed behind her...

"Good night Amina!" Troy yelled. Amina ran back inside and hugged them and kissed them, told them good night, and ran back over to us...

"Good night Uncle Troy, good night Auntie Keisha!" they all said in unison as they left. When they got inside Beautiee leaned into Bazil and held him...

"You okay?" Bazil asked...

"I'm okay – I'm just tired..."

"C'mon – let's get you upstairs..." Bazil said as he picked Beautiee up and began carrying her up the stairs...

"When I get married I'm gonna carry my wife upstairs like Daddy..." Jay said...

"Me too!" Joseph said as they followed Bazil and Beautiee upstairs. When they got upstairs, Bazil carried Beautiee into the bedroom and laid her on the bed...

"You okay Mommy?" Lydia asked...

"Mommy's tired..." Beautiee yawned...

"Mommy go to sleep?"

"Mommy go to sleep..." Beautiee yawned...

"C'mon – let's get ready for bed..." Bazil said as the kids followed him to their rooms. After they were settled he came back into the bedroom... "Beautiee?"

"Yes Bazil?"

"Are you okay?"

"I'm okay..."

"What's wrong?"

"I got a bad feeling..."

"About what?"

"This whole situation..."

"Really?"

"I hope it doesn't keep them from getting married..." Beautiee sighed...

"Come here..." Bazil said as he pulled her up into his arms and held her... "You're really worried about them?"

"Bazil... this isn't going to end well..." she whispered as she drifted off to sleep...

Chapter 20 – Fritz & LaShonda

They barely made it in the door before Fritz went in on LaShonda... "You had to ruin it..."

"What'd I do?"

"You know damn well what you did – don't act like you don't know what the fuck I'm talkin' about!"

"Fritz! Don't you dare talk to me like that!" she snapped...

"Do you even like Lexi?"

"How could you ask me that?"

"You barely spoke to her – you didn't congratulate her – and don't think I'm blind – I saw how you were looking at Sterling!"

"How was I looking at Sterling?"

"Well – since you asked – you were looking at him like you wanted what they had..."

"Fritz! That's not true! We have what they have! I love you! I want you!"

"Yea okay – that's why we have sex once or twice a month right?"

"I'm sorry – we can have sex more often if you want..."

"It should be what you want LaShonda!"

"It is! I promise!"

"You were rude to Natasha for no reason – even after she apologized – and don't even get me started on the way you tried to go at Beautiee..."

"Beautiee? You're mad because I asked her about her books?"

"Keep actin' like you don't know what I'm talkin' about..." Fritz mumbled. LaShonda went over to Fritz and kissed him...

"Let's go to bed... I'll make it up to you..."

"You don't need to make it up to me – you need to make it up to them..."

"I want to start by making it up to you..." she breathed as she slid down onto her knees and unzipped his pants...

"Shonda... don't..."

"Why not?" she asked as she began stroking his dick...

"Shonda..." Fritz moaned as she took his dick in her mouth. LaShonda literally had him in the palm of her hands as she grabbed his ass and pushed him in further... "Shonda... Shonda... Shonda..." he moaned as he grabbed her head with his hands and fucked her mouth...

"Mmmf... Mmmf... Mmmf..." she moaned on his dick...

"Shonda... Shonda... I'm cummin... I'm cummin... Uuuggghhh!" LaShonda swallowed and then she got up off her knees, wrapped her arms around his neck, and kissed him...

"Better?"

"Much better..." he breathed as he kissed her...

"C'mon – let's go to bed..."

"Okay..." Fritz said as he took her by the hand and they went into the bedroom. When they got inside Fritz took off his clothes and climbed into bed. LaShonda took her clothes off, got in bed beside him, and began kissing him on his neck...

"LaShonda... I'm tired..."

"Fritz... I'm horny..."

"I need... sleep..." he yawned as he drifted off to sleep...

"I knew I shouldn't've sucked your dick!" she snapped as she got up and went into the bathroom. She turned on the shower, stepped in, and allowed the water to beat down on her for a few moments. After the water got good and hot, she reached for the body wash, squirted some into her hands, and rubbed it all over her body... "Sterling..." she whispered as she rubbed and squeezed her breasts. She moved her hands down her body and when she got to her pussy, she put one leg up on the tub and began rubbing her clit with one hand while finger-fucking herself with the other... "Sterling..." she moaned as her orgasm began building...

"LaShonda?" Fritz yawned. When he turned over and realized she was in the shower, he got up and decided to join her...

"Sterling... Fuck me..." she moaned as she increased the pressure on her clit and on her g-spot...

"LaShonda?"

"Sterling... yes... fuck... I'm cumming!" LaShonda continued playing with her clit and finger-fucking herself as she experienced mini orgasms... "Huh... Huh... Huh... Huh... Oh shit... Sterling... Fuck... I'm cumming again... Aaaaggghhh!"

"Was it good?" Fritz asked as he snatched the shower curtain open...

"Fritz! Fuck! You scared the shit outta me!"

"Sorry 'bout that..." he lied... "I woke up... I had to pee... didn't mean to scare you..."

"How long were you in here?" she asked as she got out and began drying off...

"Not long..." he lied...

"I'm going to bed – you coming?"

"I'll be there in a bit..." he answered...

"Okay..." she said as she gave him a kiss and left the bathroom. Fritz put the blower on, closed the bathroom door, sat on the toilet, put his head in his hands, and cried...

Chapter 21 – Sterling & Lexi

"Sterling! I'm cumming! Aaaggghhh!"

"Lexi... Lexi... Lexi... Fuck! Uuuggghhh!" I collapsed on top of Lexi while I was still inside her and began kissing her...

"Sterling..."

"Lexi..."

"I... need... to... get... up..."

"No..."

"Sterling..."

"No..."

"I... need... Oh God – get up!" she yelled as she pushed me off her, jumped up, and ran to the bathroom...

"Lexi..." I whispered as she hurled into the toilet. I went over to the sink, wet a washcloth, wiped her forehead, wiped her face, and helped her stand up...

"I'm sorry..."

"Stop that..." I said as I picked her head up by her chin and kissed her...

"Sterling... let me..."

"Stop that..." I said as I kissed her again...

"Okay..." she sighed...

"Are you okay?"

"I think so..."

"It's too soon for you to be pregnant..." I laughed...

"I think I over-did it on the seafood..."

"That's okay – how are you feeling?"

"I'm better..."

"C'mon – I'll make you some tea..."

"I think I can handle coffee..." she said as she followed me back into the bedroom...

"Lexi – I'm going to make us some coffee and bring it into the living room..."

"The living room?"

"Yes – I want us to talk..."

"Are you upset with me?"

"No..." I answered as I put on my robe and slippers and went into the kitchen...

"Hello..." Lexi answered...

"Hi Lexi – it's Beautiee..."

"Hi Beautiee!"

"I got your number from Natasha – I hope you don't mind..."

"I don't mind..."

"I was calling to ask if you needed any help with planning the wedding..."

"Oh wow – I wasn't thinking about it – but now that you mention it – I could use a friend..."

"Is everything okay?"

"Everything's fine... but..."

"Lexi – what's wrong?"

"I don't want LaShonda at my wedding..."

"Did you tell Sterling that?"

"Yea..."

"What'd he say?"

"He said we don't have to invite them..."

"So what's wrong?"

"He wants Fritz..."

"Lexi – he said you didn't have to invite them – right?"

"I just want him to be happy..."

"Lexi – all he needs is you..."

"Okay..."

"Bazil asked me to marry him and we went to Vegas and got married..."

"Vegas? How was it?"

"It was everything..."

"Did you have pictures?"

"I found a package that included a limo for the bride, the groom, city hall, the ceremony, pictures, video, and a chapel..."

"Oh wow..."

"When Bazil's daughter got married, I helped her plan her wedding too..."

"Oh wow..."

"I gave birth to our first child on her wedding night at the Taylor Inn Bed and Breakfast in Boston...

"Oh my God!"

"I was in labor at the reception and she helped me give birth – along with her mother..."

"What?! Okay – how did that happen?"

"I'll tell you more about that the next time we get together..."

"I'd like that..."

"I can go with you to David's Bridal and help you pick out stuff too – and guess who my best friend is?"

"Who?"

"Keisha!"

"Keisha? Keisha Cochran?"

"Yup!"

"Oh my God!"

"I'll let you go – these kids wanna eat – save my number – and tag me in the pictures!"

"Okay Beautiee – thanks!"

"You're welcome..." Beautiee said as she hung up...

"Who were you talking to?" I asked as I came into the living room with the coffee and set it on the table...

"That was Beautiee..."

"Oh that's nice – how's she doing?"

"She offered to help me plan our wedding and help me pick out stuff at David's Bridal..."

"That's nice! I'm glad you two hit it off..."

"Me too..."

"Were you serious about working with me?"

"Yes..."

"Well – if you're serious – it's going to require a lot of time..."

"Okay..."

"The best route for you to take is to become a massage therapist..."

"I can't be a personal masseuse like you?"

"Yes – you can – but you need to become a massage therapist first..."

"Will I need a license?"

"Absolutely..."

"How do I get my license?"

"You have to complete a massage therapy program, you have to get certified by the state, and you need to get a degree..."

"I need to go to college?"

"Yes..."

"How long do I have to go to school?"

"That's up to you – you can go full-time and get it done before four years..."

"Oh wow..."

"You have to take classes in medical terminology, body mechanics, massage ethics, anatomy, and physiology..."

"It sounds like I'm studying to be a doctor..."

"You need to complete all the practical requirements. You also need hands-on experience..."

"Where do I get that?"

"You do an internship at a massage clinic..."

"Oh..."

"After you complete your internship, you need to pass the licensing exam for massage and body work. Those exams are administered by the Federation of State Massage Therapy Boards..."

"This is a lot..."

"Do you still want this?"

"Yea..."

"Okay – after you pass those exams you can apply for a state license and complete a certification..."

"Okay..." she sighed...

"You'll need 125 hours of body systems anatomy, physiology, kinesiology, and 40 hours of pathology..."

"What's...?"

"Anatomy is bodily structure of humans and animals – pathology is cause and effect of disease or injury – kinesiology is the study of the mechanics of body movements..."

"That's a lot..."

"We're not done..."

"Oh my God!"

"You'll need 200 hours of supervised instruction and 10 hours of business and ethics..."

"This is a lot..."

"That's why we get paid like we do..."

"Where do I start?

"The Cortiva Institute has a campus in Hartford. After you complete your courses you can do your 200 hours of supervised instruction and your internship with me..."

"How can I do that when you don't have a location?"

"Let me worry about that..." I said as I leaned forward and kissed her...

"I love you..."

"I love you too..."

"I guess I better start looking for a job..."

"You'll be exhausted if you try to work a full-time job and go to school full time..."

"I can apply for financial aid..."

"You won't qualify..."

"I don't have any income..."

"You don't... but your husband does..."

"Sterling – I need to pay for school..."

"Lexi..." I said as I stood up and pulled her up and held her... "There are two things you need to do...

"Okay..."

"First..." I breathed as I kissed her... "You need to let me make love to you again..."

"Mmm... okay..."

"Second..." I breathed as I kissed her again... "You need to let me take care of everything else..." I said as I picked her up in my arms and carried her into the bedroom...

Chapter 22 – Fritz & LaShonda

"Shit!" LaShonda exclaimed as the water started running out the toilet and onto the floor...

"What's wrong?!" Fritz exclaimed as he jumped up outta bed...

"The fucking toilet's clogged!" LaShonda yelled...

"Move!" Fritz commanded as he pushed LaShonda out the way and dropped down on his knees...

"What are you doing?!" Fritz ignored her question and turned off the valve behind the toilet...

"Thank you..." LaShonda breathed...

"You're welcome – get me a bucket and some towels..."

"Okay – I'll be right back..." she said as she hurried into the kitchen, got the bucket from under the sink, and ran back to the bathroom...

"Where's the towels?"

"I'll be right back..." she said as she hurried over to the linen closet and pulled out as many towels as she could hold and then she handed them to Fritz...

"I'll clean this up – you call the plumber..."

"Okay..." she said as she went to go call the main office...

"Front desk..."

"This is Mrs. Aubert..."

"Yes Mrs. Aubert – what can I do for you?"

"Do you have a plumber available?"

"We have the suppa – what seems to be the problem?"

"Our toilet's clogged..."

"Have you shut off the valve in the back?"

"My husband did..."

"Okay – I'll send the suppa right up..."

"Thanks – but I think we need a plumber..."

"We'll send the suppa first – if he can't fix it then we'll get a plumber..."

"I think I should just get a plumber..."

"That's fine – but I have to inform you that you'll be responsible for any damages to other tenants..."

"What if there are damages from the suppa?"

"There won't be – trust me..."

"Okay..."

"Shall I send him up?"

"Please..."

"Okay – I'll send him right up..."

"Did you call the plumber?" Fritz asked as he came out the bathroom...

"The front desk is sending the suppa..."

"I hope he can fix this..." Fritz sighed...

"I'll go make coffee..." LaShonda said as she went into the kitchen...

"Who is it?" Fritz asked...

"Suppa..." Fritz opened the door and looked him up and down...

"Good morning – my name is Earl..." he said as he extended his hand...

"Mr. Aubert..." Fritz said as he shook Earl's hand...

"I'm here to fix your toilet – may I come in?"

"Yes – of course..." Fritz said as he opened the door...

"Good morning..." LaShonda said as she came into the living room with two cups of coffee...

"Good morning Mrs. Aubert – that coffee sure smells good..."

"Would you like some coffee?" she asked as Fritz rolled his eyes...

"Let's find out what's going on with your toilet..." Earl said as he went into the bathroom with his tools. Once he got in the bathroom he pulled his snake out and proceeded to run it down the toilet...

"How's it going?" Fritz asked as he came in to observe...

"I'll let you know in a sec..." Earl gritted as he pushed the button to reverse so it would come out the toilet...

"What the hell is that?" Fritz asked as he looked at what appeared to be white rocks at the end of the snake...

"Oh my God! What the hell is that?" LaShonda asked as she came to the bathroom...

"Condoms..." Earl answered...

"Condoms? What the hell are they doing in my toilet?" Fritz asked...

"Well Mr. Aubert... that's where they go when you flush them..." Earl answered...

"That's odd – I don't use condoms..."

"You don't?"

"Nope..."

"Well... they could've come from the tenants upstairs – but one thing you should never do is flush condoms down the toilet – it's considered kryptonite to plumbing – especially in apartment complexes..."

"Oh wow..." Fritz said...

"When you flush condoms down the toilet they form giant balls – like the ones you saw – they trap odors and create massive blockages in pipes, plumbing, and sewers..."

"So you should throw condoms in the garbage?" LaShonda asked nervously...

"Absolutely – I'm going to make sure your toilet is working properly before I leave – and then I'll go upstairs and check their toilet..." Earl said as he went back to work...

"I'm going out for a minute – I'll be right back..." Fritz said as he went out the door...

"Mrs. Aubert – you're all set..." Earl said as he came out the bathroom..."

"Thank you Earl..." LaShonda sighed...

"You're welcome..."

"Can I give you a cup of coffee to go?"

"Sure – thank you..."

"I'll be right back..." she said as she went into the kitchen. Earl waited for her to come back with the coffee and when she did, he took a sip right away... "Good huh?"

"Very..." Earl acknowledged...

"Have a good day..."

"You too – and thanks again..." Earl said as he left their apartment and ran right into Fritz... "Oh my God – I'm so sorry!" he exclaimed...

"Don't worry about it – listen – I need to go with you when you check the apartment upstairs..."

"I can't let you do that Mr. Aubert – I could lose my job..."

"Please – I think my wife's cheating on me..." Fritz sighed...

"Oh my God... I'm sorry..."

"So am I..."

"I'll tell you what – you come upstairs with me – if they're home I'll tell them I need to check their bathroom because you're on the same line..."

"What if they're not home?"

"I'll let you know what I find..." Earl said as they both went upstairs. When they got upstairs, Earl knocked on the door...

"We have a problem..." Sterling read the text message and sat with the phone in his hand for a few moments before he replied...

"Who is this?"

"LaShonda..."

"Why are you texting me?"

"The suppa just left here..."

"And you're telling me this because?"

"I'm telling you this because our toilet was clogged from the condoms you flushed..."

"Are you sure it was me?"

'My husband doesn't use condoms..."

"Are you sure it was me?"

"You're the only other man I've been with..."

"I'm sorry about your toilet..."

"We'll have to come up with an alternative..."

"An alternative?"

"For when you come see me next week..."

"Are you fucking crazy?!"

"What's wrong?"

"I'm engaged to Lexi..."

"So what?"

"So you really think I'm going to fuck you ever again in life?"

"That's exactly what I think – in fact – that's what's going to happen – it'll be your gift to me..."

"My gift to you? For what?"

"For not telling your fiancée..."

"Haah! She already knows!"

"You're lying!"

"You wanna talk to her?"

"I wanna talk to you... and then I want you to fuck me... without a condom..."

"Okay – I'll fuck you..."

"Thank you – shall I see you next week?"

"You won't see me at all – but what you will do is continue to pay me – it'll be my gift to you..."

"How the fuck is that a gift to me?"

"As long as you continue to pay me... I won't tell your husband..."

"I'm not paying you shit!"

"Fine with me – oh – before I forget – thank you for our engagement party! Aaah Haah!"

"Fuck you mutha fucka!"

"Mr. Carpentier – I need to check your toilet..." Earl said as Mr. Carpentier opened the door...

"Mr. Aubert – what are you doing here?" Mr. Carpentier asked...

"Our toilet was clogged earlier from condoms being flushed..." Fritz answered...

"Condoms? Well they didn't come from me – my wife and I are trying to have a baby..."

"Congratulations..."

"Thank you..."

"Mr. Carpentier – can I come in and check your toilet?" Earl asked...

"As long as you're not accusing me of causing trouble..." he laughed...

"I'm not – it's just that you're on the same line..."

"Sure – c'mon in..." Mr. Carpentier said as he opened the door and they both went inside...

"Is your wife at home?" Fritz asked as Earl headed to the bathroom...

"No – she gets up and out early..."

"Where does she go so early?"

"She likes to go for a run on the path before it gets crowded..."

"Oh wow..."

"Mr. Carpentier – you're all set..." Earl said as he came out the bathroom...

"Did you find any condoms?"

"I didn't find anything but water..." Earl answered as he headed towards the door...

"Have a nice day..." Mr. Carpentier said as he held the door open for them to leave...

"You too..." they both said in unison as they left...

"Where'd you go?" LaShonda asked as Fritz came in the door...

"I went for a walk on the path..." Fritz lied as he walked past her, sat down at the desk, and started going through the mail. LaShonda shrugged her shoulders and went into the bedroom...

Chapter 23 – Fritz

"$18,000?! What the fuck!" Fritz exclaimed when he saw the American Express bill... "Let me take a look at this..." he said as he looked at the charges... "Sterling Enterprises... $1,000... Once a week every week since March?! Okay..."

"Thank you for calling American Express – this is Shonda – may I get your name?"

"Aaah Haaah! Aaah Haaah!"

"Sir – what's so funny?"

"I'm sorry!" Fritz laughed... "It's just that my wife's name is LaShonda and I call her Shonda..."

"Your wife must be really special..."

"Oh she's special alright..."

"Mr. Aubert?"

"Yes – this is Mr. Aubert – how'd you know?"

"The number you're calling from is associated with your account..."

"That's what I'm calling you about..."

"Is there a problem?"

"Absolutely..."

"Are you calling to report your card stolen?"

"No – I'm sure my wife's responsible for the charges..."

"Would you like me to remove her from this account?"

"You can do that?"

"I sure can..."

"Thank you – I'd like that..."

"I get lots of calls from husbands..." she laughed...

"Is that right?"

"Oh yes..."

"I can get you a new card, but it will have the same account number..."

"I can't get a new account number?"

"I can't do that unless you file your card as lost or stolen - if you report your card stolen, you won't be responsible for the charges..."

"So you lose out on $18,000?"

"Don't worry about that – you report the card stolen – we'll investigate the charges – at the end of the investigation Sterling Enterprises will have to reimburse us – unless they can prove they didn't know the card was stolen..."

"Sigh... it wasn't stolen..."

"Are you sure?"

"I'm sure..."

'Okay... let me ask you another question..."

"Okay..."

"Is it possible your wife's card was stolen?"

"I don't think so..."

"You're not really sure though – are you?"

"No... I'm not..."

"Okay – I'll take care of the report – I'll close out this account and we'll re-issue another card for you alone – is there anything else I can help you with?"

"Could you give me an address for Sterling Enterprises?"

"Hang on a sec... okay – the address is 87 East Broadway, Unit D, Milford, CT 06460..."

"Thank you! You wouldn't happen to have a phone number – would you?"

"860-712-7300..."

"Thank you Shonda!" Fritz exclaimed...

"Thank you for what?" LaShonda asked as she came in...

"I'm on the phone..." Fritz answered...

"You're all set – you should have your new card in 10 days – have a great day..."

"You too..." Fritz said as he hung up...

"Who was that?" LaShonda asked...

"It was work – I gotta go – I'll be back later..." Fritz said as he jumped up from the desk, shoved the American Express bill in his jacket, and went towards the door...

"I'm going inside to lay down..." LaShonda said as she gave Fritz a quick kiss, dropped her cell phone and pocket book on the table, kicked off her shoes, and went into the bedroom...

"Hmmm... let me see if you have Sterling's number in your phone..." Fritz said out loud as he picked her phone up. When he saw the text message she sent to Sterling he was livid... "I'll just forward this to myself, delete it, and put your phone right back where it was..." he said as he forwarded the message to his phone, deleted it from her phone, put her phone back on the table, and went out to the parking lot. When he got in the car, he closed the door and began reading the text...

"We have a problem..."
"Who is this?"
"LaShonda..."
"Why are you texting me?"
"The suppa just left here..."
"And you're telling me this because?"
"I'm telling you this because our toilet was clogged from the condoms you flushed..."
"Are you sure it was me?"
'My husband doesn't use condoms..."
"Are you sure it was me?"
"You're the only other man I've been with..."
"I'm sorry about your toilet..."
"We'll have to come up with an alternative..."
"An alternative?"
"For when you come see me next week..."
"Are you fucking crazy?!"

"What's wrong?"

"I'm engaged to Lexi..."

"So what?"

"So you really think I'm going to fuck you ever again in life?"

"That's exactly what I think – in fact – that's what's going to happen – it'll be your gift to me..."

"My gift to you? For what?"

"For not telling your fiancée..."

"Haah! She already knows!"

"You're lying!"

"You wanna talk to her?"

"I wanna talk to you... and then I want you to fuck me... without a condom..."

"Okay – I'll fuck you..."

"Thank you – shall I see you next week?"

"You won't see me at all – but what you will do is continue to pay me – it'll be my gift to you..."

"How the fuck is that a gift to me?"

"As long as you continue to pay me... I won't tell your husband..."

"I'm not paying you shit!"

"Fine with me – oh – before I forget – thank you for our engagement party! Aaah Haah!"

"Fuck you mutha fucka!"

"C'mon Fritz – snap out of it..." he said out loud as he turned on the GPS...

"Location please..."

"87 East Broadway, Milford, CT 06460..."

"Here are the directions..."

"Thank you..." Fritz said as he followed the directions and went straight to my house. When he got to the parking lot he parked the car, turned off the engine, and waited... "Hello Lexi..." he said as he picked up his phone, zoomed in on her at the beach, and started recording... "Your fiancé is a lucky man..." he said as he recorded Lexi in her bikini applying sunscreen on her arms and legs... "I wish it were my hands all over you..." he said as he zoomed in on Lexi's stomach and moved down to the top of her pubic area... "Damn I wanna fuck you..." he breathed... "This will work..." he said as he stopped recording... "Now – let's see where you are..." he said as he pulled up the GPS and typed in the phone number...

"Call or Location?"

"Location..."

"Location is 1125 Windward Road, Castle Cove Marina..."

"Thank you..." Fritz said as he smiled a sinister grin to himself and drove to Castle Cove Marina...

Chapter 24 – Kenique (Nique)

"Hey my Thirst Quencher..." she breathed as she wrapped her arms around my neck and kissed me fully...

"Hey..." I breathed. I always looked forward to seeing Nique. She has Lexi's caramel complexion and beautiful jet black hair that cascades down her back to her ass. She is a beautiful woman from Barbados and her accent turned me on whenever she spoke...

"Would you like to something to drink?" she asked as she stepped back, allowing me to admire her nude body...

"No thank you..." I answered, smiling mischievously...

"What would you like?"

"I'd like to please you..." I answered as I walked over to her, picked her up in my arms, carried her into the bedroom, and laid her on the bed...

"Take off your clothes..." she commanded...

"As you wish..." I said as I began to undress slowly...

"Come closer..." I went over towards the bed and she sat up on the bed and opened her legs. I stood between them and Nique began to unbuckle my belt... "There you are..." she said as she unzipped my pants and slid them off my ass along with my boxers...

"Yeesss..." I moaned as she took my dick in her mouth. I always enjoyed it when Nique sucked my dick because she enjoyed it as much as Lexi – maybe even a bit more. Unlike a lot of men I know – I never thought that a woman that enjoys giving oral pleasure was considered a whore – there's a difference between sucking dick for a buck and sucking dick because you want to give pleasure to someone you care about without judgement or guilt – and Nique was giving me the pleasure she wished she could give her husband but couldn't...

"Are you ready?" she asked as she looked up at me...

"I'm ready..."

"Come to me..." she commanded as she lay back on the bed, positioned herself on the pillows, and spread her legs. I climbed on the bed, got in between her legs, put the dental damn on my tongue, and flicked her clit... "Oohhh..." she moaned. I swirled my tongue around her clit a bit until she began squirming and I saw her wetness between her legs...

"Tell me what I can do for you..." I said as I got up on my knees and put on the condom...

"You can finish what you started..." she answered...

"As you wish..." I said as I got back down between her legs, spread them wide, and dove in...

"Fuck!" she moaned. She was sopping wet so it was slippery and sloppy just like she liked it... "Oh God! Yes! That's it! Right There!" Once she grabbed my head with her hands I knew she was close to cumming so I grabbed her legs, pulled her clit to my nose, and shook my head back and forth... "Yessss! I'm cumming! Aaaggghhh!" I continued swirling my tongue around her clit as long as her body trembled and until her orgasm subsided... "Thank you... I needed that..." she breathed...

"My pleasure..." I said as took the dental dam off my tongue, I came up between her legs, took her left nipple in my mouth, and sucked it gently as I massaged her breast with my hands...

"Ooohhh... yes..." she moaned. I moved over to the right breast and sucked her nipple gently as I massaged it and teased her by putting the tip of my dick on her clit... "Please..." she breathed...

"As you wish..." I breathed as I eased myself inside her. I knew she wanted me to fuck her – and I was going to – but I wanted to make love to her first...

"Please... Fuck me..."

"Ssshhh..." I whispered in her ear as I kissed her neck, lifted her legs, and pushed my dick in further...

"Please ... my Thirst Quencher... Fuck me..."

"As you wish..." I growled as I began pounding her pussy...

"Yes! Fuck me! Just like that! Fuck!" I lifter her legs up, lifted her up off the bed by her ass, and finished her... "Aaagh! Don't stop! I'm cumming! I'm cumming! I'm cumming!" Nique loved it when I came right after her and I was more than happy to oblige...

"Uuuggghhh! Uuuggghhh! Uuuggghhh!" We both lay there basking in orgasmic afterglow for a few moments. As happy as I was, I also dreaded telling her what I had to tell her... "Nique..." I whispered as I pulled the condom off and closed my hand around it...

"Yes my Thirst Quencher?" she asked as she touched my face...

"I can't see you anymore..." At first she didn't say anything – she just continued to touch my face lovingly...

"Who is she?"

"How'd you know?"

"What other reason could you possibly have for not wanting to see me?" she breathed as she kissed me...

"Thank you..." I said as I got up and started getting dressed...

"Can I ask you something?"

"Sure..."

"Will you miss me?" I didn't answer her. I finished getting dressed, turned to look at her one last time, and smiled. Once I got out into the hallway, I went over to the nearest trash can, dropped the condom in it along with the dental dam, got in the elevator, and made my way to Bazil's office...

"Gotcha!" Fritz said out loud as he recorded me leaving the building, started the car, and began following me...

Chapter 25 – Sterling & Bazil

"Osgood Publishing..." Fritz said as he waited for me to get out the car and go inside...

"Who is it?" Bazil asked...

"It's Sterling..."

"Come in!"

"Hey!" I said as I walked in...

"Hey Sterling – how are you?"

"I'm a little hungry..."

"C'mon – we'll go down to the cafeteria..." Bazil said as he got up...

"Lead the way..." I said as I followed Bazil out his office and down the hall... "This is nice..."

"Thank you..." When we got to the cafeteria, I was in awe...

"Mr. Osgood – what can I getcha?" Jack asked...

"Jack – this is Sterling – Sterling – this is Jack..."

"Nice to meet you sir – what can I getcha?"

"Egg-white omelet with onions, peppers, mushrooms, and tomatoes..."

"You want toast with that?"

"Yes please..."

"White, wheat, rye, or multi-grain?"

"Multi-grain..."

"Coming right up..."

"We'll get coffee while we wait..." Bazil said as he got himself some coffee...

"You have hazelnut?"

"Sure do..."

"Great..." I said as I made my coffee...

"Ready!" Jack called out...

"Thanks Jack..." I said...

"I'll take the coffee to a table..." Bazil said as I went to get my breakfast. After I got my breakfast, I went to sit down with Bazil...

"Ooohhh..." I said as I tasted it...

"Jack's good..."

"Damn sure is..." I agreed...

"How's things with Lexi?"

"Couldn't be better..."

"Aww..."

"Beautiee called Lexi yesterday..."

"She did?"

"She offered to help Lexi plan our wedding..."

"I'm glad they hit it off..."

"Me too – Lexi was really happy to talk to her..."

"We found out our best friend went to school with your wife..."

"Really? What's her name?"

"Keisha..."

"Keisha Cochran?"

"That's her..."

"Oh wow!"

"Let's go back to the office and I'll let you know why I asked you to come by..."

"Okay..." I said as I got up from the table... "Jack – that was delicious!"

"You're welcome..." Jack said as we left the cafeteria. When we got back to Bazil's office, he didn't waste any time...

"How long are you planning to keep doing what you're doing?"

"I'll be done on Wednesday..."

"Lexi really loves you..."

"I know..."

"It's not every day a woman knows who you really are and loves you anyway – women like Lexi and Beautiee only come along once in a lifetime..."

"I know..."

"Do you Sterling?"

"Bazil..."

"You should've stopped this a long time ago – and what the fuck were you doing with LaShonda?"

"I fucked up!" I exclaimed as I threw up my hands...

"Sterling – relax – I have an opportunity for you..."

"You're offering me a job?"

"No – but if you take me up on this offer I'll refer my employees to you – and I'm sure you'll give them a nice discount..."

"I'm listening..."

"A Touch of Bliss is thinking of filing for bankruptcy..."

"The massage spot in West Hartford?"

"That's the one..."

"Why?"

"That's not important – I met with the owner last week..."

"You did?"

"I told him instead of filing for bankruptcy he should consider selling..."

"What'd he say?"

"He said for me to give him a call as soon as I find a buyer..."

"Me?"

"He's willing to let it go for $375k..."

"Oh shit! That's a steal!"

"Shall I call him and tell him he has a buyer?"

"Do I get everything that comes with the business?"

"You get the building, the products, and the employees..."

"Lexi and I were talking yesterday..."

"About the wedding?"

"About her working with me..."

"This will be a win-win for you..."

"It will..."

"So you'll do it?"

"You have the particulars?"

"Here..." Bazil said as he handed me a blue folder... "My attorney will answer any questions you have..."

"What would you do if you were me?"

"I wouldn't have met with him or asked you to come see me if I didn't think it was a good idea – but if you don't trust me – even after I recommended you to my attorney – it's cool – I understand..."

"Alright! I'm sorry!"

"Look it over and get back to me by tomorrow..."

"I'll do it..."

"You don't wanna look it over first?"

"I'll look it over when I get home – but tell him I'll do it – I can always call your attorney like you said..."

"I'll call him right now..." Bazil said as he picked up the phone... "Mr. Carre – I have news for you... yes... I have a buyer for you... uh huh... he'll speak with my attorney... okay..."

"Thank you Bazil...

"You're welcome..."

"You won't believe what happened yesterday..."

"What happened?"

"LaShonda happened..." I laughed...

"You're engaged to Lexi!"

"Let me tell you what happened..."

"Go 'head..."

"She text me to tell me her toilet was clogged..."

"What the fuck does that have to do with you?"

"She said it was clogged from the condoms I flushed down the toilet..."

"What does she want you to do about that - pay for repairs?"

"She said we need to come up with an alternative when I come see her next week..."

"Is that Bitch crazy?!"

"I reminded her I'm engaged to Lexi and she said so what!" I laughed...

"Oh yea – she's crazy..."

"I asked her if she thought I would ever fuck her again in life and she said that's exactly what she thinks – and I better see her next week and fuck her – without a condom – she said it was her gift to me for not telling Lexi!" I laughed...

"What the fuck is wrong with her?" Bazil laughed...

"So I told her okay – I'll fuck you – you keep paying me and that will be my gift to you for not telling Fritz!" I laughed...

"Please tell me you're not serious!"

"She said she's not paying me shit!" I laughed...

"I'm so glad you're done with her..."

"Me too..."

"Don't fuck this up Sterling – LaShonda's not worth it..."

"I'm not Bazil – but I need to get going..."

"Another appointment – right?"

"I'll see you later – thanks again..." I said as I got up and left...

"Bout damn time!" Fritz said as he started the car and began following me...

Chapter 26 – Laverne

"Oh Shit! Laverne? Aaah Haah Haah! Aaah Haah Haah!" he laughed as he started recording... "I ain't mad – I guess somebody gotta hit your ole ass – better him than me!" he laughed as he watched me get out the car and walk up to Laverne...

"Hey my Thirst Quencher!" she squealed...

"Please keep your voice down!" I exclaimed...

"Why I gotta keep my voice down?!" she snapped as she turned around to face me with her hand on her hip...

"Because..." I said as I pulled her close to me... "I'm your Thirst Quencher between the sheets..." I breathed in her ear...

"You're right... I'm sorry..." she said as she ran her hand between my legs. This was going to be a challenge for me today – especially after seeing Nique earlier – but I had to be nice. Older women always required special attention – and if you didn't make them feel like they meant something to you – they'd bite your head off – they didn't give a damn who heard them...

"I'm going to help you upstairs with your groceries..." I said as I picked up her bags... "I'm going to cook for you..." I said as I closed the trunk... "We're going to eat..." I said as I turned to face her... "And then I'm going to make love to you..."

"Okay..." she breathed as she gave me a quick kiss and we headed upstairs to her apartment. I could barely get in the door before she pushed me back against it, forced her tongue in my mouth, and unbuckled my belt...

"Laverne... wait..."

"I can't – I'm so horny – I need your dick – now!" she exclaimed as she reached in my pants and pulled my dick hard. I couldn't stand it – but this was my job – and today was payday – so I did what I had to do...

"You missed this dick huh?" I growled as I pushed her down on her knees...

"Yes my Thirst Quencher – yes!"

"Show me..." I breathed as she unzipped my pants and took my dick in her mouth. Thank God I could close my eyes and imagine Lexi sucking my dick – otherwise it would've been an epic fail. Don't get me wrong – she had skills – her suction was amazing – I didn't know if it was because she didn't have any teeth in her mouth or not – but between her skills and my imagination I was rock hard...

"Yes... I love it..." she said between sucking and slobbing. I couldn't stop thinking about Lexi and I instinctly grabbed her head by both hands to play in her hair... and her wig came off...

"Shit! Hole on!" she exclaimed as she took her mouth off my dick to pick up her wig...

"Leave it..."

"Hell no – ain't no man ever seen my bald head but my husband!"

"Laverne... leave it..." I said as I helped her up...

"I didn't want you to see me like this..." she said as she teared up...

"Stop that..." I said as I kissed her tears... "You're a beautiful woman..."

"You goin' mess around and make me fall in love with you..." she laughed...

"You don't need to wear a wig..."

"This ole bald head – oh no – I needs a wig..."

"No..." I said as I kissed her again... "You just need someone to see you and love you for who you really are..."

"You full o' shit..." she laughed...

"Laverne – don't ever say that to me again..."

"I'm sorry..."

"Your natural hair is beautiful..." I said as I ran my hand across her head and played in her curls...

"Really? I was thinking of dying it..."

"What color were you thinking about?"

"I bought some brown dye..."

"Let me get dinner started and then we'll dye your hair if you want..."

"You'd do that for me?"

"Who am I?"

"My Thirst Quencher..."

"Let's get this started..." I said as I picked up the groceries and she followed me into the kitchen. I waited for her to sit down and then I started to take my clothes off. Once I was completely nude, I took everything out the bag, washed my hands, and began prepping to cook. Laverne didn't care for black-eye peas, neck bones, chitterlin's, or pig feet so I never had to worry about being nauseous – her favorite was meatloaf au jus, mashed potatoes, and collard greens so I was good to go...

"It's so nice to have someone cook for me..." she said as I began cleaning the collards...

"Your husband never cooked for you?"

"Oh no – he said cookin' and cleanin' was women's work...

"Some of our greatest chefs are men..." I said as I pre-heated the oven to 350...

"My husband always said a man that cooks doesn't have a woman to cook for him..."

"That's true in some cases..." I said as I prepped the meatloaf. Once I got it prepped, I put the collards to the side and peeled the potatoes...

"You always do that so fast..."

"A peeler cuts the time in half..." I said as I continued. Once I was done with the potatoes I put a pot of water on the stove, cut them up, and dropped them in the water. I took the collard greens, placed the leaves in in stacks, rolled them into a cigar, and cut across them to make strips. I took out a cast iron skillet and added olive oil, the collards, some salt, and let them simmer as I put the meatloaf in the oven. After the collards started browning, I added garlic, turned the flame down, and let them continue to simmer. The potatoes were ready so I poured the water off of them, mashed them up, seasoned them with ranch seasoning and butter, and covered them...

"That smells so good..." she sighed. I walked over to her, stood in front of her and watched as she admired my body...

"Come with me..." I commanded as I extended my hand. Laverne took my hand and I led her to the bathroom... "Take off your clothes..."

"Yes my Thirst Quencher..." she said as she stripped out of them quickly...

"Do you have any Vaseline?"

"Yes... but..."

"Go get the Vaseline..."

"Yes my Thirst Quencher..." she said as she went into the bedroom. When she came back into the bathroom I sat on the toilet and opened the Vaseline... "Spread your legs..."

"What you fixin' to do?"

"Who am I?"

"Yes my Thirst Quencher..." she said as she spread her legs and I began applying Vaseline to her labia... "I'on know what you doin' – but I like it..." I continued applying Vaseline to her labia and the surrounding area but I didn't apply any to her public hair...

"Where is the hair color?"

"I'll get it..." she said as she got it and handed it to me. I was relieved when I saw Overtone Coloring Conditioner because that meant there was no pre-mixing, no dripping, and no harsh chemicals...

"Uh uh! What you doin'?!"

"Have I ever done anything to hurt you?"

"No..."

"Okay then..." I said as I went back to applying the conditioning color to her pubic hair. Once I was done, I stood up, put her in front of the mirror, stood behind her, and let her watch me put the coloring conditioner on her hair...

"That feels good..." she breathed as I massaged her scalp. I continued to apply the coloring conditioner to her hair while simultaneously massaging her scalp and she started moaning... "Ooohhh... That feels good... Yes..." Once she closed her eyes, I knew she was going to enjoy what was coming next...

"Turn on the shower..."

"Yes my Thirst Quencher..." she breathed as I took a condom out of the medicine cabinet and put it on...

"Get in..."

"Yes my Thirst Quencher..." she breathed. Once she got in the shower, I got in behind her and began to rinse the coloring conditioner out her hair... "Ohhh... That feels good..." I continued massaging her scalp, making sure all the coloring conditioner was rinsed out and then I got the shampoo and washed her hair. After I was done washing her hair I pulled her to me, slid my dick inside her from behind, and washed her public hair as I began thrusting... "Ohh... Yes... Gimmie that dick... Yes... Just like that!" Laverne braced herself against the wall and I bent her over a little as I continued pounding her pussy... "Oh God – you 'bout to make me cum – don't stop – I'm cummin'... I'm cummin'..." I grabbed her hips and slammed my dick in her as she reached her climax... "AAAGH! AAAGH! AAAGH!" I continued slamming my dick in her as her legs shook and then she caught me by surprise - she pulled herself off my dick, dropped down in the tub, took my dick in her mouth, and when she pulled my dick out her mouth she spit the condom out... "Fuck my mouth!" she commanded. I was in shock – in a good way – and I was happy to oblige as I grabbed her head with both hands and did as I was told...

"Uuugh! Uuugh! Uuugh! Uuugh! Uuuggghhh!" Laverne swallowed every drop and then she stood up, pulled me to her, and kissed me... "Let's go in the bedroom – I need to show you something..." I said as I turned off the water...

"Okay!" she squealed as she got out, I got out, we both dried off, and then we both hurried into the bedroom...

"Look at yourself in the mirror..."

"I done seen myself naked plenty..."

"Look at yourself in the mirror..."

"Oh my God..." she whispered as she teared up...

"How do you like it?"

"You made me look so beautiful..."

"God made you beautiful..." I breathed as I kissed her and moved my hand down between her legs and across her public hair...

"Every time I look in the mirror I'm going to think of you..."

"Put on your robe – let's go eat..."

"Okay..." she breathed. After she put her robe on, we went into the kitchen. As I made the plates, I began dreading the conversation I knew I had to have with her... "This looks so good..."

"You're welcome..." I said as I placed the plates on the table, got two forks, and sat down...

"This is so good!" she exclaimed...

"I have to tell you something..."

"What's wrong?"

"I can't see you anymore..."

"What'd I do?"

"I'm engaged to be married..."

"Congratulations... I guess..."

"Thanks..."

"I ain't mad – you needs you a wife – I'm gonna miss you though..."

"I'm gonna miss you too..."

"Really?"

"Yes – my other clients only want one thing from me – you're different..."

"I'on know about that..."

"You are – you always tell me how much you appreciate me when I cook for you..."

"I didn't know it meant that much to you..."

"It does..."

"I hope I find me a man like you..."

"You will..."

"You just sayin' that to be nice..."

"Laverne – stop that..."

"Okay..."

"I want you to make me a promise..."

"Okay..."

"Promise me you'll look at yourself in the mirror everyday..."

"I promise..."

"Promise me you'll remember how beautiful you are..."

"I promise..."

"I gotta get going..." I said as I got up and started getting dressed. Laverne didn't say anything. After I got dressed, I started to walk towards the door and she pulled me into a kiss. I held her for a few moments and then I left. As I headed downstairs, I could hear her crying...

"Finally!" Fritz exclaimed as he started the car and began following me home...

Chapter 27 – Sterling & Lexi

"Hey my Thirst Quencher..." Lexi said as I walked in..."

"Hey..." I sighed as I walked past her and went straight into the bedroom. I knew Lexi felt bad but I couldn't talk to her yet. I took off my clothes, dropped them in the hamper, and went into the bathroom. I locked the door to make sure Lexi wouldn't come in because if she did, I wouldn't have been able to resist her...

"Sterling – open the door..." she said as she tried to open the door and couldn't..."

"No..."

"Sterling... please... talk to me..."

"I'll be out in a minute..." I said as I turned on the water and stood underneath it. I took my time in the shower and all I could think about was Laverne crying when I left. I wanted to get out the shower and open the door but I thought better of it and stayed in the shower a bit longer...

"Sterling?"

"Yes Lexi?"

"Come and talk to me... please..."

"I'm coming Lexi..." I sighed as I turned off the water and got out the shower. I dried off completely before I unlocked the door and opened it. Lexi was standing there completely naked...

"Come here..." she said as she took my hand and led me to the bed. Lexi sat down on the bed against the headboard, spread her legs, and held her arms open. I sat down on the bed and Lexi turned me away from her... "Lay back..." I lay back against Lexi and she held me against her without saying a word. Lexi breathed on my head and I could feel the warmth of her breath on my scalp as she ran her hands up and down my arms and across my chest...

"It's over..."

"Ssshhhh..." Lexi whispered as she kissed my head and began massaging my shoulders. I closed my eyes and enjoyed what she was giving me. As I relaxed a bit more, Lexi applied more pressure as she continued massaging my shoulders and then she began moving down my arms. I slid down, Lexi slid up, and before I knew it, she was ass up on top of me. I wanted to grab her by her ass and push her pussy down on my face, but Lexi pinned my arms down at my sides as she continued massaging them. Lexi moved her hands to my hips and then she moved her hands down my thighs as she continued massaging them. When she got to my legs, she stretched out on my body and continued massaging as my dick pressed up against her. When she got to my feet, Lexi massaged one foot at a time and then she did something no other woman has ever done to be before – she took my big toe in her mouth and sucked it as she continued massaging my foot...

"Ooohhh... Lexi..." I breathed. Lexi moved over to the other foot and began sucking my big toe as she massaged my other foot... "Ooohhh... Lexi..." I breathed as she hit erogenous zones I didn't know existed. Lexi got up on her knees, moved back on my body until her ass was within reach of my mouth, and then she took my dick in her mouth... "Lexi... Fuck!" I moaned as she pinned my arms back down at my sides. Lexi was torturing me purposely by taking me all the way in her mouth and then slowly taking her mouth off my dick while swirling her tongue around it and when she moved her hands to massage my thighs again, I grabbed her by her ass, spread her cheeks, and showed no mercy...

"STERLING!" she screamed as I licked and sucked her asshole. Lexi took my dick back in her mouth and quenched my thirst as I slid my tongue in her ass, up her crack, down to her pussy, and back up to her asshole again... "Mmmph... Mmmph... Mmmph..." The sounds Lexi was making had me turned up, thirsty, and hungry and as I slid my tongue back down to her pussy she began bucking on top of me as I thrust my dick up into her mouth... "MMMPH!

MMMPH! MMMPH! MMMPH!" Lexi was shaking as she came in my mouth and was relentless as I continued sliding my tongue up her ass, in her asshole, down her pussy, in her pussy, and around her clit... "MMMPH! MMMPH! MMMPH! MMMPH!" Lexi was sucking my dick with so much purpose she used her hands to support herself on my thighs and this time when she took me all the way in her mouth down to my balls I erupted...

"UUUGGGHHH!" I held Lexi down on my face and continued licking and sucking, alternating between her ass and her pussy until she stopped sucking my dick and then I turned her over on her back, grabbed her by her ass, lifted her up off the bed, and ran my tongue up and down from her pussy to her ass while shaking my head back and forth...

"STERLING! OH GOD! FUCK!" she screamed as she grabbed my head with her hands and fucked my face as her legs shook... "AAAGGGHHH!" I rolled on my side, turned Lexi's body so her pussy stayed in my face, and we fell asleep...

Chapter 28 – Fritz & LaShonda

"Where have you been all day?" LaShonda snapped as Fritz walked in...

"Take off your clothes..."

"Excuse me?"

"Don't make me repeat myself..." he said as he went into the bedroom and got undressed. LaShonda went in the room behind Fritz and began taking her clothes off... "Come over here – let me look at you..."

"Okay..." she said as she stood in front of Fritz and took off her panties...

"Lay on the bed..."

"Okay..."

"Spread your legs..."

"Okay..." she said as Fritz started stroking his dick...

"Le'me see that pussy..." LaShonda spread her legs and spread her lips... "Play with it..." LaShonda began playing with herself as Fritz continued stroking his dick... "How's it feel?"

"It... feels... good..." she moaned...

“Squeeze your tits...” he commanded as he took out his phone and started recording...

“Fritz... No...”

“Fuck yourself...” he commanded. LaShonda pushed her fingers inside her pussy and began finger-fucking herself...”

“How does that feel?”

“It... feels... good...” she moaned...

“Make yourself come like you did in the shower...”

“Fritz... Please... Fuck me...”

“I will... but I want you to make yourself cum like you did in the shower...” he said as he continued recording. LaShonda took her fingers out her pussy and began swirling her fingers around her clit...

“Fritz... Please... Fuck me...”

“I’ll fuck you... but I need you to cum for me first...”

“Fritz... Ooohhh... Ooohhh... Fuck...”

“That’s it... give it to me...” Fritz commanded as he continued recording...

“I’m cumming... I’m cumming... I’m cumming...”

“How’s it feel?”

“It’s good... It’s good... Ooohhh... Fuck... I’m cumming again...”

“Cum for me Shonda...” Fritz commanded as he got up on the bed, held the phone with one hand, and began finger-fucking her with the other...

"Fritz! Fuck me! Oh God! Don't stop! Aaaggghhh! Aaaggghhh! Aaaggghhh!"

"That's it Shonda... Let me see it..." he commanded as he kept recording...

"It feels so fucking good! Don't stop! Fuck me!" she screamed as she bucked up and down on Fritz's hand while simultaneously rubbing her clit...

"Yes Shonda... your pussy's so wet... give it to me..."

"Aaaggghhh! Aaaggghhh! Aaaggghhh!"

"How's it feel baby?"

"Oh Fritz... Fuck... I needed that..." she breathed...

"I know..." he said as he stopped recording, put the phone down, and started stroking his dick again...

"Bring it to me..." LaShonda breathed. Fritz stood at the end of the bed and LaShonda scooted down to the edge and took his dick in her mouth...

"Yes... Suck it..."

"You like it Daddy?"

"Yes... That's it... Suck it..." Fritz was good and hard and when he came close to busting he stopped LaShonda... "Get on your back..." LaShonda got on her back, Fritz got on the bed, put LaShonda's legs up on his shoulders, thrust himself inside her, and began pounding her pussy...

"Fritz! Fuck Me!" LaShonda screamed...

"Lexi... Lexi... Lexi... I'm cumming... Uuuggghhh!"

"Get the fuck off me!" LaShonda screamed as she started crying...

"Don't make me stop now Lexi – your pussy feels so good... Uuugh! Uuugh! Uuugh!"

"Stop it!" LaShonda screamed...

"Oh Lexi..." he breathed as he put LaShonda's legs down and continued stroking... "I've been waiting to fuck you ever since I saw you at the beach..."

"Get the fuck off me!" LaShonda screamed as she pushed Fritz off her...

"Lexi..." he breathed as he kissed her... "What's wrong?"

"Don't you ever call me Lexi!" she screamed as she slapped him...

"Didn't you call me Sterling the other day when you were masturbating?"

"Oh my God!"

"That wasn't God..."

"I can explain..."

"When I got up to come in the bathroom I didn't have to pee – I wanted to join you and make love to you... but... once I heard you call his name..."

"I'm sorry..."

"What exactly are you sorry for?"

"I'm sorry for making you feel the way you made me feel when you called me Lexi..." she sighed...

"You broke my heart..." Fritz whispered as he sat on the bed and tears streamed down his face...

"Fritz – please... Don't cry... I'm sorry..."

"Are you sorry because you were caught or are you sorry because you mean it?"

"I mean it – I swear – it'll never happen again..."

"Is that because you don't want it to happen again or is that because Sterling told you he wasn't ever fucking you again in life?"

"Oh my God... how did you..."

"Come with me – I have something to show you..." he said as he took LaShonda by the hand, snatched her off the bed, and pulled her into the living room... "Sit down!" he commanded. LaShonda sat down on the couch and Fritz threw the American Express bill in her lap... "Open It!" LaShonda took the bill out the envelope and read it over as her hands shook...

"I'm... I'm..."

"Shut up!"

"I'll pay it..."

"Oh please – with what – that bullshit you do at David's Bridal?"

"I'll come work at IBM..."

"I have something else to show you..." Fritz said as he played a video and handed her his phone...

"Sterling is at Castle Cove Marina – so what?"

"He went to see another one of his clients..."

"So what? Why are you showing this to me?"

"I just want you to see he doesn't give a fuck about you..."

"I don't care about this!" LaShonda exclaimed...

"No? Okay – take a look at this one..." Fritz said as he snatched the phone from her, played another video, and showed it to her...

"Oh my God! Is that Laverne?"

"Yea..."

"No!"

"I waited for nearly two hours..."

"Oh my God – I can't believe he's fucking Laverne!"

"I can't believe he's fucking you..." Fritz sighed...

"I'm sorry..."

"No you're not..."

"Fritz..."

"You knew you were fucking him when you invited them to dinner – you knew you were fucking him when you stood up to take pictures – you knew you were fucking him when we came home and we had that argument – and you still want him to fuck you – at least that's what you said in your text – let me read it back to you in case you forgot what you said..." and then he pulled out his cell phone and started reading the text message...

"We have a problem..."
"Who is this?"
"LaShonda..."
"Why are you texting me?"
"The suppa just left here..."
"And you're telling me this because?"
"I'm telling you this because our toilet was clogged from the condoms you flushed..."
"Are you sure it was me?"
'My husband doesn't use condoms..."
"Are you sure it was me?"
"You're the only other man I've been with..."
"I'm sorry about your toilet..."
"We'll have to come up with an alternative..."
"An alternative?"
"For when you come see me next week..."

"Stop it! I've heard enough!" LaShonda cried...

"Wait – I haven't gotten to the best part!" Fritz said as he continued reading...

"Are you fucking crazy?!"
"What's wrong?"
"I'm engaged to Lexi..."
"So what?"

"So you really think I'm going to fuck you ever again in life?"

"That's exactly what I think – in fact – that's what's going to happen – it'll be your gift to me..."

"My gift to you? For what?"

"For not telling your fiancée..."

"Haah! She already knows!"

"You're lying!"

"You wanna talk to her?"

"I wanna talk to you... and then I want you to fuck me... without a condom..."

"Okay – I'll fuck you..."

"Thank you – shall I see you next week?"

"You won't see me at all – but what you will do is continue to pay me – it'll be my gift to you..."

"How the fuck is that a gift to me?"

"As long as you continue to pay me... I won't tell your husband..."

"I'm not paying you shit!"

"Fine with me – oh – before I forget – thank you for our engagement party! Aaah Haah!"

"Fuck you mutha fucka!"

"Fritz... please..." LaShonda whispered as she started crying. Fritz ignored her and went into the bedroom. LaShonda listened to the closet doors opening and the drawers slamming and she knew what was coming next... "Where are you going?" she asked when she saw him with the suit case..."

"I have one more thing to show you..." he said as he took out his phone, played another video, and gave her the phone...

"Is that Lexi?"

"Yes it is..."

"Oh my God... you were watching her? Why?"

"I was trying to figure out why he wanted all these other women when he has a beautiful woman waiting for him at home..." he answered as he took his phone away from her, put it back in his pocket, picked up the suitcase and walked out the door, slamming it behind him...

Chapter 29 – Sterling & Lexi

"Lexi?" I called out. I looked around the room and I didn't see her but I smelled coffee so I knew where she was. I got up, put on my robe and slippers, and went into the kitchen...

"Aww... I wanted to surprise you..." I went over to Lexi, grabbed her, and kissed her hard... "Wow! What did I do to deserve that?"

"That was for last night..." I breathed and this..." I breathed as I kissed her again... "Is for this morning...

"I don't know what got into you last night... but oh my God..."

"You got into me Lexi..."

"I did..." she sighed as she picked up two cups of coffee and placed them on the table...

"Let me get that..." I said as I went to go get the plates...

"Uh uh – go sit down..."

"Okay..." I said as I went to sit at the table...

"This looks delicious..." I said as she put the plates on the table...

"I hope you like it..." she said as she sat down...

"Scrambled eggs, turkey sausage, potatoes, fruit, buttermilk biscuits – I love it..." I said as I tasted the eggs... "Ooohh!"

"You like the eggs?"

"Mozzarella & white cheddar..."

"Yes!"

"Thank you..."

"You're welcome..."

"It's over..."

"I know..."

"Lexi – it's over..."

"What time are you going out today?"

"I'm not..."

"I thought you said it would be over by Wednesday?"

"I don't want to be with anyone else but you..."

"You mean it? Is it really over?"

"Bring me my phone..."

"Okay!" she squealed as she went to get my phone and hurried back into the kitchen. I took the phone from Lexi, put it on speaker, and started making phone calls...

"This is Trenice..."

"Hello Trenice..."

"Hey my Thirst Quencher..."

"I'm calling to let you know I won't be able to see you anymore..."

"Oh no – why?"

"I'm engaged to be married..."

"You sure you wanna get married? It didn't work out too well for me..."

"I'm sure..."

"Lose my number!" she snapped and then she hung up...

"Ouch!" Lexi laughed as I dialed the next one...

"Good morning..."

"Good morning Corrine..."

"Hey my Thirst Quencher!"

"I'm calling to let you know I won't be able to see you anymore..."

"Stop playing..."

"I'm engaged to be married..."

"Click..."

"Oh my goodness!" Lexi laughed as I dialed the next one...

"This is Barbara..."

"Hello Barbara..."

"Hey..."

"I can't see you anymore..."

"Why not?"

"I'm engaged to be married..."

"Congratulations – I'm at work – bye!" she said as she hung up...

"What is wrong with them?" Lexi laughed as I dialed the next one...

"Good morning – this is Shirley..."

"Good morning Shirley..."

"Hey my Thirst Quencher – this is a nice surprise..."

"I can't see you anymore..."

"You could 'a told me that in person..."

"No I couldn't..."

"Why not?"

"Because I'm engaged to be married..."

"How you gonna feel when somebody fucks your wife like you been fucking other men's wives?"

"Good bye Shirley..." I sighed as I hung up... "I'm sorry Lexi..."

"It's over now..."Lexi said as she touched my hand...

"I love you..."

"I love you too..." she said as I called the next one...

"Good morning..."

"Hello Shelby..."

"Sterling – did we have an appointment?"

"I can't see you anymore..."

"I'm sorry – can I re-schedule for another time?"

"I'm engaged to be married..."

"That's great – have a good day..." she said as she hung up...

"What was that about?" Lexi laughed...

"Her husband was there..."

"Ooohhh..." she said as I dialed the last one...

"Good morning..."

"Hello Samantha..."

"Hey my Thirst Quencher..."

"I can't see you anymore..."

"I understand..."

"You do?"

"Look – it was fun while it lasted – don't worry about me – I'll be fine..."

"Take care Samantha..."

"You too..." she said as she hung up...

"Oh my God... it's really over..." Lexi sighed...

"Lexi – listen to me..."

"Okay..."

"If you need anything – please tell me..."

"Sterling – I have everything I need..."

"After we finish breakfast – I want us to talk..."

"About yesterday?"

"Yea..."

"I wanted to talk to you yesterday..."

"I know..."

"Let's finish eating..." she said as she picked up my phone...

"What are you doing?"

"Deleting contacts..." she answered as she continued scrolling through my phone. I smiled to myself as I watched Lexi delete contacts with one hand while eating with the other... "Fuckin' Bitch!"

"What's wrong Lexi?"

"Why do you still have this text message?" she snapped as she turned the phone to me and showed me the text...

"Sigh... I thought it was funny..."

"Really Sterling?! What's so funny about this?! Huh?!"

"I thought it was funny that she still expects me to fuck her after everything that happened..."

"What?!"

"Lexi – did you read it?"

"I stopped reading after I read what she said about coming up with an alternative..."

"Finish reading it..." Lexi read the rest of the text and then she put her head in her hands...

"I'm sorry..."

"You don't owe me an apology – I owe you one..."

"No you don't..."

"Yes I do – I should've deleted it..."

"I'm glad you didn't..."

"You are?"

"Yea..."

"Why?"

"I knew she never liked me..."

"Finish your breakfast..." I said as I picked up my phone and deleted the text. Lexi and I finished our breakfast without saying a word. I got up from the table, put the dishes in the dishwasher, and went back over to the table... "C'mon..." I said as I took Lexi by the hand and we went into the living room... "Sit down – I have something to show you..."

"Okay..."

"I went to see Bazil yesterday..." I said as I sat down next to her and picked up the folder off the table..."

"How's he doing?"

"He's fine – he found out A Touch of Bliss was filing for bankruptcy..."

"Sounds like a spa..."

"That's exactly what it is..."

"Okay..."

"Bazil reached out to the owner and convinced him to put the business up for sale instead of filing for bankruptcy..."

"That's a good idea..."

"I thought so too – that's why we're buying it..."

"We are? We're going to have our own spa?"

"Yes Lexi..."

"Oh Sterling!"

"We're stepping into a business that's already been built – we don't have to look for a location – we don't have to hire employees – we don't have to build inventory – and the best part is – you can get your supervision and hands-on experience with me..."

"I love you so much..."

"I love you too – I'm going to look over these papers but I already told Bazil I'd do it..."

"How much does the owner want?"

"He wants $375k..."

"Wow! That's a lot of money!"

"That's actually a steal..."

"It is?"

"He was considering bankruptcy – after the business is turned over to me he has to settle with his creditors – by the time he pays them he won't have any money left..."

"What if he owes back taxes?"

"I'll have to pay those at closing..."

"Do you have that kind of money?"

"Would I even consider doing this if I didn't?"

"No..."

"Exactly – I'm going to call Bazil and tell him we're doing this – and then I want you to get dressed so I can take you to West Hartford and show you where we'll be working..." I said as I picked up the phone to call Bazil...

"Okay!" Lexi squealed as she jumped up and ran into the bedroom...

"Good morning Sterling...

"Lexi's on board..."

"Okay! I'll call Mr. Carre and let him know so you can make this happen..."

"Thank you Bazil..."

"You're welcome..." Bazil said as he hung up. I heard the shower and smiled to myself as I got up and went to join Lexi...

www.ingramcontent.com/pod-product-compliance
Lightning Source LLC
Chambersburg PA
CBHW072124170626
46813CB00004B/1680
9781734335361